"We're too different, Reece,"

Lanie said. "Your life is orderly, from *A* to *B* and all the way down to *Z*. My life is alphabet soup. When I wake up each morning, I never know what I'll find in my spoon." She laughed wryly. "And this morning I found *you*."

"Look," Reece said. "Don't you think you're making a big deal out of nothing? I agree with you that it's ridiculous to even think about us . . . starting something . . . together. Sharing a couple of little kisses doesn't make us lovers." He looked at her. "But there's no reason we can't be friends."

Just like there's no reason I can't be president of the United States, she thought.

"Umm, I seem to have forgotten my manners," Lanie said. "You were very kind to come over and help me last night. Thanks . . . *friend*."

"That makes us even. I forgot to thank you for risking getting the stuffing kicked out of you the other day. Thank *you*, friend." He leaned over and kissed her lightly. "See, nothing to it."

Dear Reader,

It's February—the month of love! And what better way to celebrate St. Valentine's Day than with Silhouette Romance.

Silhouette Romance novels always reflect the magic of love in compelling stories that will make you laugh and cry and move you time and time again. This month is no exception. Our heroines find happiness with the heroes of their dreams—from the boy next door to the handsome, mysterious stranger. We guarantee their heartwarming stories of love will delight you.

February continues our WRITTEN IN THE STARS series. Each month in 1992, we're proud to present a book that focuses on the hero and his astrological sign. This month we're featuring the adventurous Aquarius man in the enchanting *The Kat's Meow* by Lydia Lee.

In the months to come, watch for Silhouette Romance books by your all-time favorites such as Diana Palmer, Suzanne Carey, Annette Broadrick, Brittany Young and many, many more. The Silhouette Romance authors and editors love to hear from readers, and we'd love to hear from *you*.

Happy Valentine's Day . . . and happy reading!

Valerie Susan Hayward
Senior Editor

CAROLYN MONROE

Kiss of Bliss

Best wishes!

Carolyn "Monroe" Greene

Silhouette ❦ *Romance*

Published by Silhouette Books New York

America's Publisher of Contemporary Romance

To the memory of James Weatherford, who taught me to see the funny side of life, and to Laura Weatherford, for passing along the writing gene.

And to Floyd, my own special country boy, who proved that opposites *do* attract.

 SILHOUETTE BOOKS
300 E. 42nd St., New York, N.Y. 10017

KISS OF BLISS

ISBN: 0-373-08847-7

First Silhouette Books printing February 1992

Printed in the U.S.A.

ACKNOWLEDGMENTS

I am grateful to the members of Richmond Writers' Bloc and Virginia Romance Writers for their suggestions and encouragement before, during and after the creation of *Kiss of Bliss*. I especially thank:
Leanne Banks—for being there day in and day out, through all the fun and agony;
Liz Henley—for laughing in all the right spots;
Cynthia Holt—for knowing *Kiss of Bliss* would see print, even when I wasn't sure;
Janet Evanovich—for showing me it's okay to break the rules.

CAROLYN MONROE

lives within spitting distance of Flat Rock in Powhatan, Virginia, with her fire fighter husband and two terrific children. Carolyn used to write feature articles for the local newspaper; she now prefers fiction to nonfiction because she can make up the facts. She has received awards for her writing, but better than that, she has received checks. Carolyn is a member of Romance Writers of America and the Virginia Romance Writers.

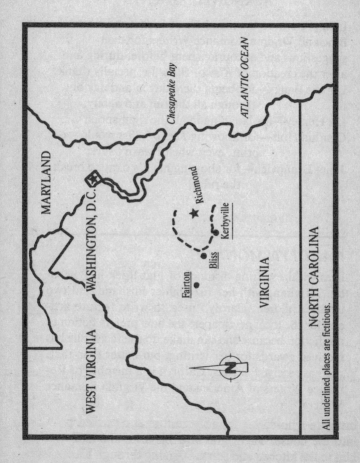

MARYLAND

WASHINGTON, D.C.

WEST VIRGINIA

Chesapeake Bay

ATLANTIC OCEAN

Richmond

Kerbyville

Bliss

Fairton

VIRGINIA

NORTH CAROLINA

N

All underlined places are fictitious.

Chapter One

"**Q**uick, gimme your gravy strainer!"

No *hello* or *glad-to-meet-you*. The frantic woman just stood there in Reece's doorway, her hand outstretched in expectation, her dark pageboy hairstyle falling in disarray around her delicate face. Something resembling a black dog hid behind her legs... very attractive legs, at that. Come to think of it, she looked even better up close than when he'd watched her through his bedroom window earlier, as she'd mowed the grass next door.

He promptly forgot the paperwork he'd been doing and stuck out his hand in greeting. "You must be my new neigh—"

"Don't just stand there—we've got lives to save!" The brunette ignored his friendly gesture and pushed past him into the house. Then, grabbing his arm, she half dragged him to the kitchen and started digging through his cabinets. The floor grew cluttered with piles of pots and baking pans in her wake. "Here's a colander," she said, shoving the thing into his arms, "but the holes are too big. Where's your gravy strainer?"

What was with this woman? At her impatient prodding, he racked his brain for an answer. "Umm…" Reece pushed a lock of hair off his forehead. What had he done with that thing after he'd filtered the oil in his tractor?

"How about a flour sifter?" she persisted. When he hesitated to consider what a flour sifter might be, she snapped her fingers under his nose. "Hurry, before they all die!"

Reece's clumsy search through the cabinets finally turned up a sifter as well as the misplaced strainer.

"Thanks a million," exclaimed the human hurricane as she slipped out the back door with her bounty. She popped her head back in. "C'mon, I need your help."

It didn't dawn on him to ask why. Even if he tried, he probably couldn't squeeze a word in sideways. Well, what the hell. She had aroused his curiosity. Reece shrugged and jogged barefoot after her across his lawn to her backyard. He caught up with her at the rail fence and gave her cute bottom a boost across the wood structure. Then he followed her to a small, collapsible pool where she dipped out a bucketful of scummy water.

She set the bucket on the ground and pointed to a hole in the side of the pool. From the hole trickled water and little round black things. On closer inspection, he saw that the black things wriggled in a puddle on the ground.

"My mower tossed a rock through the side of this thing. The tadpoles will die if we don't do something quickly." She held the strainer to the hole and tried to catch the slippery creatures. "Damn—pardon me. This isn't working."

Reece forced his eyes off the sight of her, kneeling in mud and pawing frantically at the flow of water. Mumbling under his breath about *Save-the-Whale* types and about women in general, he pulled off his T-shirt which read, If

You're Not Hungry, Thank A Farmer, and stuffed it into the hole. He picked up the flour sifter and started scooping out the hapless creatures and transferring them to the bucket.

To his surprise, the woman sat cross-legged, the back of her tie-dyed shorts planted squarely in the mud. Something about her labeled her as different from hometown girls. Obviously a city girl, Reece decided. Not New York kind of city. No, she didn't seem sophisticated or haughty the way he imagined a metropolitan woman to be. But she was sidewalks and streetlights, apartments and buses.

She seemed unaware of ruining her clothes, she was so intent on capturing, in her bare hands, the tadpoles squirming in the puddle before her. Not many girls he knew would voluntarily touch a live tadpole. Or a dead one, either, for that matter. In fact, he didn't know many girls from Bliss County who'd willingly trade places with the one beside him.

"There." She triumphantly plunged her hands into the bucket and washed the mud and tadpoles from them. "The worst of the crisis is over. Thanks for your help." Reece couldn't help noticing how the smile reached her greenish brown eyes even before her lips turned up. "I'm sorry I acted so rude before. I get carried away sometimes." He could easily visualize men in white suits hauling her away.

She held out her hand, made a face at the scum and bits of grass clinging to her fingers and large amethyst ring, and wiped the gunk on the front of her shirt. She examined her hand and, satisfied that it was clean enough, stuck it out toward Reece once again. "I'm Lanie, and I just moved in yesterday."

Reece put down the sifter and took her hand in his. Although her bone structure was small, almost fragile, she gripped his hand firmly.

"My name's Reece." He let his eyes wander over her lush figure and noticed she was perusing his bare chest just as thoroughly. "Welcome to Bliss." Indeed, the day was seeming more blissful by the minute. He had to admit she improved the scenery immensely.

Water gurgled in the bucket behind Lanie. Her pet had plunged its muzzle up to its eyeballs in the water and was slurping greedily.

There was something about the animal that commanded his attention. Reece stared. It wasn't a dog after all. In fact, it looked like a tiny, knee-high horse.

"Cripes, Winnie, that's not your water bucket." Lanie let go of Reece's hand and grabbed a handful of mane to pull the animal away. "We're trying to save those suckers, and you're *drinking* them!"

"A horse? That little thing's a horse?"

Lanie pointed the young animal in the direction of her house and swatted it on the rump to send it away from her lifesaving mission. But the horse decided, instead, to take a cooling walk in the pool.

"That does it." Apparently forgetting her mission, Lanie stepped into the pool, penny loafers and all, and picked up the horse.

Tiny hooves swung wildly in the horse's struggle to get free as Lanie walked toward the house. But it was no use. Lanie opened her back door and set the animal down, shook her finger at it as she muttered something, and closed the screen door behind her. Its squeaky bleats followed her back to the pool.

Reece shook his head. And he'd thought this was going to be another boring Sunday afternoon. "Are you going to leave him in the house to do you-know-what all over the floor?"

"You're a country boy, aren't you? Don't you know the difference between a filly and a colt?" Lanie knelt and went back to scooping the remaining tadpoles from the pool into the bucket. "Even if you didn't, Winnie is a girl's name, you know. And she's housebroken."

Reece refused to consider how someone might go about housebreaking a horse. Winnie sounded off again. He noticed that the tiny animal stood dog-style with its front feet against the door to get a better view of the goings-on outside.

"I've never heard of anyone keeping a horse in the house." He couldn't resist adding, "She'd probably be happier outdoors, where she belongs."

"Aw, hell—pardon me. You're not gonna start on that, too, are you? Hold this."

Lanie thrust the sifter into his hands and began collapsing the sides of the pool until a makeshift spout formed near Reece. He obediently held the sifter under the spout while she lifted, pouring water and tadpoles out of the pool. He dumped the batch of wriggling amphibians into the bucket, and then they repeated the process.

"I was run out of my apartment because of people with attitudes like yours," Lanie said. Her voice rose as she imitated her scorners. "My, my, dearie, don't you know livestock belong outdoors? This is a residential area, and we don't want any horses around here."

Reece again dumped the contents of the sifter into the bucket. "If you feel that strongly about it, why didn't you stay and fight?"

"Hmmph. I read about a woman in California who tried to change her zoning code to allow for a miniature horse. After she spent forty thousand dollars in legal fees, she couldn't afford her mortgage." Lanie lifted the pool higher, running the last of the water through Reece's sifter. "No thanks. I'd rather move to the country where 'livestock' is allowed.''

He stood and hoisted the bucket. "You have every legal right to keep a horse here, but I still think it's a dumb idea to let it stay in the house. I don't even let my cat come inside."

"If your cat is the gray one with the white paws, I wish you *would* keep it in your house. I found evidence of his digging in the mulch around my rosebushes."

It was plain to see the woman was raving, and Reece deemed it wise not to carry the discussion any further. She obviously couldn't see logic where her pet was concerned.

"There's a pond across the road," he said. "Let's go set these buggers free."

Lanie opened the screen door to let Winnie out, and both ran to catch up with Reece. "Mrs. Masardi's car isn't here," she said as they trudged across the neighbor's property. "Do you think she'll mind if we dump tadpoles in her pond? I met her while moving in yesterday, but I don't know her well enough to help myself to her pond."

"Don't worry, she won't mind." He knew she was almost as nuts as Lanie, except for allowing animals in the house. Reece was certain she'd gladly give the creatures a home, as long as she didn't have to share her house with them. He wondered briefly whether the increased tadpole population would attract snakes. He was preparing to give the bucket the old heave-ho when Lanie stopped him with a hand on his arm.

"Don't you dare fling those poor animals into that pond! Give me that." She took the pail from his hands and waded knee-deep into the water. She lowered the container into the water and let the pollywogs drift out into their new home. Reece heard her talking in a squeaky voice, as an adult speaks to a small child. "Come on, you poor little things.

Get those tails moving." She gently swished the water with her fingers, then looked up at Reece. "I think some of them are in shock."

Reece thought that might explain his own condition. Ever since she'd pounded on his door twenty minutes ago, his brain seemed to be moving in slow motion. As she bent over to speak to the creatures, however, her scoop-necked top dangled loosely from her body. His brain—and hormones—suddenly shifted into overdrive. Have mercy! She wasn't wearing a bra.

Seeing her state of dress, Reece did what any red-blooded Southern gentleman in his position would do. He let his eyes linger on the soft swells, drinking in the sight of the tender flesh. For one brief, insane moment, he allowed the notion of a relationship with this woman to flit through his mind.

But, no, this woman and her craziness would be bound to upset his life, his mind, and his rigidly enforced work schedule. He wouldn't let a pretty face and shapely figure jeopardize his two-year struggle to rebuild the family business. Irritated with himself for letting her distract him from going over the week's sales receipts, he snapped, "I don't have time to stand here fooling with a bunch of tadpoles. If they're not moving by now, they're probably dead."

Trying not to notice the look of hurt that betrayed her emotions, he spun on his heel and stalked back to the house.

Lanie watched him disappear over the rise toward his house. His sun-streaked blond hair had been neatly combed a short while ago. It now stuck out at various angles. He swung his arms to accommodate his long stride. As he moved, the muscles played across his bare, sun-bronzed back. Lanie recalled gaping at his naked chest, fascinated by the golden-brown hairs liberally covering it. She hoped in retrospect that she hadn't been too obvious, staring at him as she had.

All of a sudden, she realized how dopey she must look, standing up to her knees in Mrs. Masardi's pond while minnows and tadpoles nibbled at her ankles. Winnie bleated at her from shore as if to emphasize the ridiculousness of her situation. *Great, Lanie,* she thought, *you've only been here two days and you're already labeled a fruitcake.*

Too bad it had been Reece she'd blown her cover to. What a hunk! She'd thought she was going to swoon when he'd peeled off his T-shirt. If only she could have acted normal until he got to know her. But she'd ruined her chance with Reece—and set her reputation in this new community—by being herself: Zany Lanie.

Mud squished in her shoes as she slogged toward shore. Her dad couldn't have picked a more appropriate nickname to describe his eldest child. Her three younger brothers had seen their share of childish mishaps, but it had always been Lanie's antics that attracted attention. Maybe that was because, in so many other ways, she was Miss Reliable. From the time her mother had died when Lanie was five, she'd been a little helper to her father and junior mom to her brothers. Thus, when she had overdosed on Alka-Seltzer, childishly anticipating an explosive release of gases to propel her into midair, it had caused more of a stir than if one of her brothers had done the same thing.

If today was any indication, her reputation had followed her to Bliss, the place she'd chosen to live mostly because she liked the name.

"Is that you, Elaine?" Mrs. Masardi slammed the car door shut and walked toward the pond, cupping her hands above her eyes.

Lanie's feet hit dry ground, and she couldn't help marveling at her sense of timing, to be emerging from the pond like a monster from the black lagoon at the exact moment Mrs. Masardi was returning home in her Sunday best. Maybe this was God's punishment for cutting the grass on His day.

She approached her neighbor, hoping the elderly woman wouldn't hear the sucking sound in her shoes. "Uh, hi, Mrs. Masardi."

"Nice day for a cooling dip, isn't it?" The older lady walked to the patio and pulled two rocking chairs together so that they faced the pond. "Have a seat. I'll get us some iced tea and a towel for you to dry yourself."

"That's okay— I can't stay long. Gotta finish mowing the lawn."

Mrs. Masardi's eyebrow raised almost imperceptibly as she took a seat beside Lanie, but she said nothing.

"Th-that's why I was in your pond."

The other eyebrow came up to match the first.

"My mower threw a rock through the side of a child's pool that had been left in my backyard—"

"Oh, yes, the Eastwoods. They were the former owners. The pool belonged to their two small children. They've been gone about two months now."

No wonder her yard had looked like a jungle. Lanie went on to explain how hundreds of helpless tadpoles were at risk of dying if she hadn't removed them from the leaking pool. Rather than implicate Reece, who already seemed perturbed with her, she decided it best to leave his name out of her description of the scenario. She would take full responsibility for dumping the tadpoles in Mrs. Masardi's pond.

"I hope you don't mind, Mrs. Masardi. I didn't know what else to do."

"Please don't call me Mrs. Masardi. It makes me feel like an old woman." She reached over and patted Lanie's arm. "My name's Dot." Then, as if to prove that they were now on casual terms, she kicked off her low-heeled shoes and propped her feet on the redwood table. "As for those tadpoles, I think it's a wonderful thing you did. You're a sweet girl, Elaine."

Lanie pondered whether to mention it had been Reece's suggestion in the first place.

"Where do you work, dear?"

"Nowhere right now. I had a secretarial job until recently. Unfortunately my father died a few months ago, and I missed a lot of time from work to settle his affairs. Since I was still on my probation period, they let me go."

"Oh, my."

"That's okay," Lanie reassured her. "I'm a good secretary, so I won't have trouble finding another job, even if it's only for a temporary agency." She spoke with more assurance than she felt. After losing the last job, not to mention her experience at the previous one, she wasn't so sure.

Winnie *tap-tapped* across the brick patio and rubbed her wet nose on Lanie's elbow. Lanie affectionately tugged the animal's forelock.

"How are you with accounts receivables and payables?"

"I made A's in bookkeeping at the community college."

"That's wonderful! You're an answer to my prayers." Dot clapped her hands together in delight.

Winnie misunderstood the gesture and helped herself to a comfy spot on the woman's lap. Dot cradled the animal and pushed a toe against the patio to set the chair rocking.

"I think I've got the job for you," Dot continued. "Mine!" At Lanie's quizzical expression, Dot rushed on. "For the past two years since my Albert passed on, I've been helping my son run the family business. But I just can't keep up a full-time job anymore, especially now that I'm...over forty." She winked and whispered conspiratorially, "Besides, I've met a gentleman friend I'd like to spend more time with." She cuddled Winnie tighter as if just thinking about her friend gave her the urge to hug something.

"What about your son? Won't he want to interview me first?"

"Oh, heavens no. He'll be so rattled when I tell him I'm quitting, he won't have the presence of mind to interview anyone. He *can* be difficult at times, you know."

"No, I didn't know." Maybe she should back out now, before she got in too deeply. "You haven't told him yet that you're leaving? Maybe he'd rather you stay on for a while longer."

"Of course he'd rather I stay! The boy's a workaholic and, regretfully, I've let him turn me into one, as well. But *this* old horse," she thumped herself on the chest, "is ready to be turned out to pasture. I want to kick up my heels."

Bored with sitting still, Winnie wriggled in Dot's arms. The older woman rocked forward and set the animal on the patio.

"But don't you worry," Dot said. "I'll stay long enough to train you for the job. After that, I'll come in to help from time to time... as my schedule permits." Her blue eyes twinkled behind her silver-rimmed glasses.

The offer sure beat pounding the pavement. The deal was clinched when Dot cited a salary close to what Lanie had earned at her previous job.

"Be there at eight o'clock. It's at 8510 Courthouse Road, just three miles off Sanderson Road. There's a sign on the front that says Masardi's—you can't miss it."

Lanie stood and offered her hand to help her neighbor up, but Dot merely shook it.

"What kind of office is it?" Lanie asked.

"It's not an office, it's a retail store."

Lanie started to say more, but Winnie distracted her by heading for Dot's orange zinnias. She caught the horse before it did any damage.

"Just be on time tomorrow morning. If I'm not there, ask for Maurice Masardi. But be on time," she emphasized. "He gets real cranky if you're late."

Lanie thanked Dot again and hurried home before Winnie could discover more ways to make mischief. On her way, she saw Reece, still shirtless, on his front porch. He set a pan near a small wooden structure that looked like a...a cat house? *To each his own*, she thought. She waved a friendly hello, but he glared back at her, his hands on his lean, shorts-clad hips.

"The same to you," she grumbled, and disappeared into the privacy of her house. Lanie made her way past the stack of boxes in her bedroom and hunted through the closet for her best working clothes. This Maurice guy—she pictured a man in his late forties, balding, and with a paunch the size of Kansas—must be a real bear to work with, she decided. With only one chance to make a first impression, she wanted it to be her best. Lanie wished she'd had time to interrogate Dot further as to what type of business the Masardis owned.

Aha! The yellow silk blouse and swingy purple skirt, pulled together with a batik-print bandeau belt. Her purple panty hose with the polka-dot design down the legs would complete the ensemble perfectly. She turned and scrutinized the stacks of cartons. Now, which one held the iron...?

Reece knelt on his front porch and rubbed the gray cat's lopped ear as his pet ate. "You stay away from over there, you hear?" He hitched a thumb toward Lanie's house. "She's trouble."

He didn't know what it was about the woman, but she rubbed him the wrong way. Bursting into his house and ransacking his kitchen . . . and all he could do was stare in amazement as she whirlwinded her way through his house. He hated being caught off balance like that! He vowed to make sure their paths crossed as little as possible in the future.

The phone rang, and he stepped inside to answer it. "And that dumb horse . . ." he growled as he lifted the receiver.

"I beg your pardon?"

"Nothing, Ma. I was just mumbling again." Reece opened the refrigerator and began assembling the ingredients for a super-colossal chef's salad.

"Oh. Well, here's something else to mumble about. Friday was my last day at the feed store."

"Wha . . . ?"

"Don't worry. There's this friend of mine who's a whiz with the books—"

"Ma, it's not that easy to get someone to replace you. How am I going to find somebody who can do the paperwork and who doesn't mind lifting fifty-pound sacks of grain when needed?" He pictured a tottering old white-haired woman trying to hoist a sack while maneuvering her walker.

"Hmm. I forgot to mention that."

Reece sighed into the phone.

"I'm sure that'll be no problem, dear. She looks like she has plenty of heart."

On the other hand, if she was anything like his mother, she'd outwork them all. "Ma . . ."

"She's starting tomorrow at eight, and you'd better be nice to her, young man! I'll be in shortly afterward to start training her." She chuckled softly. "It'll be nice to sleep late tomorrow."

There was no arguing with his mother when she started the "young man" stuff. "I wish you'd given me more time, so I could have found someone on my own."

"Maurice Albert Masardi, I gave you a year's notice." Now she was hauling out the big guns, calling him by his birth name. She might as well have pulled his ear like she'd done when he was a kid. "It took us a year to straighten out the mess your daddy left of the store when he died, but this past year has been spent *building* the business." Her voice softened. "We're in the black, honey. You don't need me anymore."

Reece stopped demolishing the lettuce. "I'll always need you, Mom."

A muffled sound came over the phone. When Dot spoke again, her sergeant's voice came through loud and clear. "My friend starts work tomorrow. Be nice to her!"

"Yes, ma'am." Reece hung up the phone and looked at the mound of salad he'd prepared. His appetite gone, he wondered what to do with it all.

The next morning Lanie checked her reflection in the bathroom mirror. Superb! She didn't consider herself much of a looker; her fair skin burned easily, and her brunette hair framed her small face in a simple style that bordered somewhere between girlish and chic. Lanie adjusted her clunky wood necklace, satisfied that she would make a smashing impression.

She glanced again at her watch. Plenty of time. Too bad there hadn't been time to drive by Masardi's yesterday and get acquainted with the route she would take. She'd have to make do by allowing extra time to get there this morning.

Winnie's bleated protests tore at Lanie's heart as she backed out of the gravel driveway. The lead line from her pet's halter allowed plenty of room for grazing, basking in the sun, or cooling off in the shade. But Winnie was a social animal, and she craved human company.

"Hush, sweetie," Lanie crooned from the car window. "Mommy will be home soon."

Fifteen minutes later, she pulled up in front of Masardi's... *Farm and Home Supply?* No matter. It should be a welcome change from the electric company where she'd worked until last week, and the psychiatric clinic before that.

As she walked in the door, she was greeted by the sight of row upon row of grass and vegetable seed, fertilizer, grain, potting soil and a variety of farm and home gardening tools. In the left front corner of the store, beyond the tractors and riding lawn mowers, an area was sectioned off with free-standing partitions. It looked like an office, so she headed for it, hoping to find Maurice Masardi.

Lanie was rounding the corner to enter the office when a tall form appeared in the doorway. She crashed into a hard chest and bounced backward in surprise. Strong arms shot out to grip her shoulders. In the moment of recognition that followed, his fingers dug harder into her shoulders.

"You! What are you doing here?" he demanded.

Lanie stared up at Reece, her jaw slack in her fascination. When he scowled like that, his dark eyes appeared even more deep-set, like those of an eagle. His piercing gaze ripped through her, and she suddenly felt stupid, gaping back at him. Remembering the first impression she had wanted to set with the owner, she snapped her mouth shut.

"I—I'm here to work. Do you know where I can find Mr. Masardi?"

"Please don't tell me... *you're* the woman my mother hired?"

Lanie slowly nodded.

He released her and made a pathetic whimpering sound in his throat. He shook his head as if to clear it. "It's that chain letter I got last week. I knew I shouldn't have broken the chain."

"You didn't tear it up, did you?"

He blinked at her in response.

"You should never tear up a chain letter. I always just let them fall into the trash can, like it was an accident."

"My mother must be a sadist."

Lanie's eyes widened as she made the connection. "*You're Maw*-Reece?" she asked, dragging out the name. Somehow, this Adonis—in corduroy shorts and a shirt that sprouted delicious dark gold hairs where the buttons stopped at the top—didn't match her idea of a *Maurice*. She giggled.

A scowl drew his thick brows together. "I was named after my favorite uncle."

Lanie clamped her teeth on her lower lip to erase the grin from her lips. "I'm sorry. I—I mean ... I'm not sorry that you were ... named ... Oh, never mind."

Reece took a deep breath, and Lanie watched the shirt expand. She pulled her eyes away from his magnificent chest to his still-brooding face. Too bad such a great body was wasted on a grouch. He stepped aside and motioned her toward one of the two desks crowded into the tiny area. "Have a seat," he said through tight lips. "We may as well get to know each other."

Lanie sat at the desk, drawing herself as erect as possible, while Reece pulled over the other chair and straddled it backward. She refused to be intimidated by his unwelcoming attitude. Nevertheless, seeing him at such close range, with his arms folded rigidly across the back of the chair, unnerved her.

"Look," she said, sitting primly upright, "if you don't want me to work here, just say so. I can find another job easily enough," she bluffed. "Maybe even a *better* one."

He hesitated a moment, as if considering the option, then appeared to think better of it. "Aw, don't get huffy. We can use your help." He looked her over from head to toe, gnawing the inside of one cheek as he stopped at her polka-dotted legs.

Beneath his intense gaze, Lanie felt strangely under-dressed.

"You got a résumé?"

Lanie reached into her purse and pulled out the some-what wrinkled sheet of paper. Expressionless, he scanned the page.

"It says here you stayed at your last job less than six months. Didn't you like the work?"

"Oh, yes, and I'm sure my supervisor there will give you a glowing assessment of my work. It's just that—" Lanie's voice cracked, and she fought to control her emotions "—I lost a lot of time due to my father's illness and subsequent death."

Reece's hard features softened for a moment, and she detected a look of empathy. Then, she recalled that Mrs. Masardi had lost her husband—Reece's father—only two years ago. Of course he would understand. "You have my sympathy," he said softly.

Uncomfortable with the quiet, Lanie babbled on. "You'll notice I worked at the City Psychiatric Clinic for over five years. My work there was also exemplary, and I have an as-sociate's degree in business administration. As I told your mother, I made straight A's in bookkeeping."

"You don't have a reference person listed for the psychi-atric clinic."

Lanie gulped. She had hoped to bluff him past that omission. "I, uh, wish you wouldn't call them for a reference."

Reece raised one eyebrow in a gesture that duplicated his mother's expression yesterday. He peered at her, blatantly suspicious. "You weren't a . . . *patient* there? Were you?"

"No, of course not! I was the administrative secretary." She leaned back in her chair to distance herself from those knowing brown eyes. "In fact, I was even cited once for my role in calming a disturbed woman who had barricaded herself in my office and threatened us with a letter opener."

Reece waited for her to finish.

She smiled in what she hoped was a charming manner. "In case you haven't already noticed," she continued, "I tend to be a bit impulsive." Reece smiled and rolled his eyes heavenward. "Anyway, shortly before I left that job, I had dressed up as Glenda, the Good Witch of the North. You know, from *The Wizard of Oz*."

"This I gotta hear."

"It was Halloween!"

The gray cat slunk into the office, jumped onto Reece's lap and settled down to sleep.

"You let your cat come inside? I thought that was against your religion or something."

Reece rubbed the feline's lopsided ears. "He catches mice."

"Yech." Lanie shuddered at the thought of sharing her office with sharp-toothed rodents.

"So they fired you for dressing like an idiot?" She realized he was teasing her.

"No. I forgot how I was dressed and went into the locked ward to deliver some charts. I even had on a halo." Lanie fingered the clasp on her purse. "It set a patient back three months in his treatment." She sighed. "That was when I decided that working in a psychiatric clinic wasn't for me."

Maybe he should fire her before she had a chance to undo two years of hard work. Surely his mother didn't know what she was getting them into. Perhaps if he explained that the girl was a catastrophe waiting to happen... Naw, that would only make his mother more determined to "help the poor thing." And he *had* promised to be nice to her.

"Please don't misunderstand," Lanie pleaded. "I can handle any crisis that comes along." The clasp on her purse snapped repeatedly as she opened and shut it. "It's the *little* things that cause me trouble."

A regular Lucille Ball. Only with straight brown hair instead of fire-red and curly. He straightened and rubbed the aching muscles at the back of his neck. With a grimace of resignation, he opened the desk drawer and dropped her résumé in with the rest of the employee records. "Welcome to the staff, Lucy."

"My name is Lanie."

"I know."

Chapter Two

Reece introduced her to two of the three employees, and Lanie immediately liked them both. Violet, a middle-aged woman who wore her long brown hair tucked under a plaid scarf, tended the cash register and dispensed farm and animal husbandry advice to grateful customers. Howard, an elderly man with a slow gait but quick smile, assembled the new tractors and equipment for display. Both worked on an as-needed basis; part-time, or not at all during the winter, and full-time from spring through fall.

"Jonathan Pollard comes after school to run deliveries and do most of the heavy lifting," said Reece as they toured the garden area. Row upon row of sprouting cabbage plants lined the fenced cement patio where Howard swept up plant fragments and scattered soil. "We all have our own jobs to do, but most of them overlap. Everyone pitches in wherever help is needed," Reece continued.

He touched her arm to guide her around the protruding handles of a wheelbarrow. As he did so, his gaze once again swept over her. His tongue rolled across his bottom lip. "Your, uh, outfit is very attractive—for a normal office situation, that is. However, since you'll be expected to help with inventory and such, you'll probably find jeans more comfortable."

Lanie agreed with him but wished he hadn't pointed out how out of place she looked. "When Dot offered me the job, I forgot to ask about the type of business. I'll wear something more appropriate tomorrow."

They headed back inside, past a display of ropes, halters, and hoof trimmers. As Lanie paused to examine a calf-sized nursing bottle, an odd tapping and sliding sound caught her attention. She heard Violet's quiet voice and assumed a customer had entered the store. "We try to stock everything a farmer or home gardener needs," Reece said.

A gray-and-white blur streaked down the aisle past their feet. Behind the blur, Winnie was hell-bent for cat meat.

Before Lanie could grasp what was happening, Reece made a tackle dive, his hand closing around the silky strands of Winnie's tail. His big arms clamped around the tiny captive.

Reece rose slowly and turned a devil's glare on Lanie.

"Winnie, what are you doing here?" Unmindful of her silk blouse, Lanie took the naughty beast from Reece's arms. She tried to ignore the angry look her new boss bestowed on her. "What got into you?"

As if in answer to her question, soft fur wound itself around Lanie's ankles.

She looked down. Big mistake. Winnie, too, caught sight of the cat beneath them. Struggling to keep a grip on her unruly pet, Lanie pushed the cat aside with one foot.

"I think Winnie...doesn't like...ow!...your cat." Winnie's bobbing head banged against Lanie's mouth. Almost immediately she felt the lower left corner of her lip start to swell.

"So *there* you are, you little rascal!" Dot appeared at the end of the aisle, carrying a newspaper and an oversized purse. "Winnie's rather frisky, isn't she?"

Reece bent down to pick up his cat. As he rose, one white paw streaked out over his arm to smack Winnie on the nose. Reece hurried away to deposit the cat outside.

His mother tucked the newspaper under her arm and grabbed the horse's chin. With her free hand she firmly thumped its soft velvet nose. "No!"

Winnie blinked, and the kicking immediately ceased. Lanie hugged her in apology for Dot's action.

"That's much better." Dot rubbed Winnie's neck. To Lanie, she added, "Animals are a lot like children and men. You have to be firm with 'em."

When Reece returned, minus the cat, Lanie set Winnie on the floor. She smoothed her skirt, avoiding the fury in Reece's eyes. Even so, she was conscious of the muscle that twitched in his jaw.

"That horse can't stay here."

Heat rose from Lanie's neck to her ears, then closed around her cheeks. Certain her pale skin now burned a brilliant red, she looked up to respond that she would take Winnie home during her lunch hour. But his scowl was fixed on Dot! Good grief—now she and Winnie were coming between mother and son. She opened her mouth to speak, but Dot spoke first.

"Of course she can! I couldn't let the poor little darling stay at home all by herself. You could hear her crying all over the neighborhood."

Lanie blushed hotter. She hadn't realized her pet would disturb the neighbors. Winnie reached up and lipped the leather strap dangling from a bridle tacked to the pegboard display. Lanie lurched forward to rescue the merchandise from her animal's inquisitive mouth. Remembering Dot's advice, she tapped the black nose, perhaps too lightly but enough to surprise the filly. "No!"

Winnie walked away and lay down among a pile of bags marked *Fescue.*

"See, she'll be fine," Dot told her son. "Now, how have you and Elaine been getting along this morning?"

Fine, until five minutes ago, thought Lanie.

"You *have* been nice to her, haven't you?" Dot shook the newspaper under his nose.

Reece darted a glance at Lanie and nodded curtly.

"Good! Try to make it a habit." Dot grasped Lanie by the crook of her arm and started past Reece. "If you'll excuse us, we have work to do."

Reece glanced at his watch. "Ten o'clock. I'd say it's about time."

"Don't sass me, young man." Their backs were to Reece as they walked to the office, and Dot smiled at Lanie's startled expression. "Men. You gotta keep 'em in their place."

For the rest of the morning, Dot kept Lanie busy. She explained about order forms, inventory, billing, accounts payable, and payroll procedures.

"Maurice insists we keep the profit margin on sales to farmers as low as possible," said Dot. "When a farmer buys in bulk, a price difference of just a few pennies can determine whether his kids get new school shoes." She handed Lanie the receipt book.

Though she barely knew Dot's son, Lanie felt a warmth of emotion as she learned of his charitable attitude. "It's very kind of Reece to do that for the farmers."

Dot leaned back in her chair and stretched. "No," she said, shaking her head. "It's the farmers who were kind to us, especially during Albert's last year with us." She closed her eyes and stayed that way for a long moment. So long that Lanie wondered if she had drifted off to sleep. When Dot's eyes opened again, Lanie saw that they were full of pain. "My husband died of a massive brain hemorrhage."

Instinctively Lanie touched Dot's hand. "I'm so sorry."

Dot squeezed her hand in response. "About three years ago, Albert started forgetting things, making mistakes. He'd mix up orders and deliver stuff to the wrong farm, and then he'd get mad and curse the farmers for correcting him. They all knew he wasn't acting like the sweet Albert Masardi they'd always known. When he got worse, they watched out for him, bringing him back here when he took off in the truck and got lost. They even paid their full bills when Albert forgot to give me the sales slips so I could charge 'em."

Lanie thought of her own father who, just a month before he died of a quick-spreading cancer, had impulsively bought her the orphaned filly. Preoccupied with hand-feeding the fragile foal, she hadn't considered the strangeness of her normally thrifty father giving her the unusual gift and buying her three brothers a used car, a prized hunting rifle, and providing a down payment on a small house. "It must have been hard for you to see him so ill. What did the doctors say?"

"Albert wouldn't go. We didn't know until after he passed away that his behavior was caused by a series of small strokes."

Reece stuck his head in the door. "There's a chef salad in the fridge whenever you two decide to break for lunch." He started to leave, then appeared to notice Dot's newspaper, still folded on top of the other desk. "Is that today's paper?"

At his mother's nod, he sat down and helped himself to the front page. Lanie stood and stretched the kinks from her legs.

"I'll go get us that salad," said Dot. To Lanie, she added, "There's only one place close by for lunch, and the hamburgers at Etta's Eatery get tiresome real fast."

When Dot left the room, Lanie noticed that the tiny cubicle seemed more crowded with just her and Reece than it had with the three of them. Though only six or seven inches taller than Lanie's five feet five, he appeared too large for the desk. Maybe it was the shorts. His tanned, well-muscled legs looked out of place in an office setting. They looked better suited to straddling a tractor seat or a horse. His shirtsleeves were rolled up to where shoulder muscles and biceps began. A pleasing sight, to say the least. But they, too, looked out of place, with his forearms resting against the edge of the desk. No, those hard arms and big hands should be working on a car engine, or hefting bales of hay, or... wrapped around her. Lanie gasped. Where had that thought come from?

At the sound, he turned and caught her full attention fixed on him. His eyes, the color of milk chocolate, questioned then studied her. Although his hair glistened from the sun like burnished gold, his eyelashes were enviably dark, almost black.

More than the raw, physical good looks, it was his brooding silence that held her transfixed. She discerned a quiet reliability about this man. It was a trait that she—spontaneous to the hilt—strove for, but which always seemed beyond her grasp.

Acutely aware that she'd been caught staring, Lanie cleared her throat and stammered "I...uh...does that paper carry the horoscope?"

Reece leaned back in his chair and rested one ankle over his knee. A furrow formed between his brows. "You don't really believe in that stuff, do you?"

"Only when it's true. I like to see how close it comes to real life."

Reece picked up the paper and opened it. "The day's half over, but let's see how close it is." He scanned the page. "Mine says, 'Take time to smell the roses. Don't overlook a treasure.'" He half laughed, half snorted. "Right, and roses make me sneeze. What are you?"

Lanie smiled to think how literally he'd read his message. Must be an Aries. "Pisces," she answered.

"Hmm. Yours might be close. 'Put on your suit of armor—prepare to do battle.' If your horse pulls another stunt like it did this morning, you'll be doing battle with *me*." He stared at her for a long moment.

"Your cat was just as guilty." Lanie squirmed and debated whether she should help Dot with that salad, just to get away from his intense scrutiny. When Reece spoke again, his words filled the small room.

"Why didn't you get a dog instead of a little horse?"

Lanie stiffened and lifted her chin. "Dogs jump on you and run your panty hose."

His warm brown eyes swept over her, trailing down to the polka dots decorating her legs. He was doing it again. Making her feel a hunger unrelated to the lunch hour. The sensation was so new to her that she was unsure how to respond to the thoroughness of his gaze.

Dot swooshed into the room with a large salad and several small paper bowls. "I just saw the most darling sight, Elaine. Your horse is sleeping on bags of grass seed, and Maurice's cat is curled up against her neck. You'd never know they were fighting just a little while ago."

Lanie stood and moved the newspaper to make room for the food while Reece reached into a drawer for plastic forks.

"Well, damn!—Pardon me." Lanie stopped in midmotion, forgetting for the moment that Dot stood waiting for her to clear the desktop. "Isn't this just typical of my luck?" she said, tapping the front-page headline. "I moved to Bliss County to get away from the suburban sprawl, and now it's following me here!"

"What's that dear?" Dot pushed the paper aside and set her burden on the desk.

Reece heaped salad into the bowls. "She's talking about the proposed highway that would come through the eastern end of the county. They've been planning it for months." He nudged Lanie with his elbow. "Gonna suit up, Don Quixote?"

He was referring to her astrological prediction. "You betcha. I'm prepared to do battle." She traced a finger along a map of the proposed route. Her timing couldn't be worse. Merely days after she'd signed the mortgage papers on her house, she'd lost her job. And now this.

The headline said it all: *Residents, businesses split over highway issue.* She'd been so out of sorts these past few months she hadn't bothered to keep up with the news. But she would do what she could now to prevent this road from going through.

If the highway were constructed as planned, the county would be irrevocably linked to the city. The shorter travel time would lure a host of commuters, turning her rural home into a suburban bedroom community. Farmers would sell off their land to greedy developers. Lanie envisioned massive subdivisions littering the beautiful landscape of her new hometown. If the area around her developed as she imagined it might, her neighborhood, now zoned for agricultural use, could become residential. This would mean higher property taxes, a burden Lanie's tight budget would not cover.

But, worst of all, her horse wouldn't be tolerated in a residential community. Lanie had already been uprooted

once because of Winnie. She couldn't afford to move again.
And with her father gone and her brothers scattered around
the state, she was ready for some stability in her life.

"It doesn't much matter one way or the other to me. I'll
be travelling," said Dot. "I wonder what Graceland is like
at this time of year."

Reece cast a sidelong glance at his mother. He took a
bowl, doused his salad with dressing and settled into a chair.
"You can't stop progress. Anyway, I could use the larger
customer base."

Lanie couldn't believe her ears. "You've lived in this
community all your life. How can you just sit back and let
them bulldoze a highway through this beautiful county?"

Reece finished munching a forkful of salad, noncha-
lantly staring up at her as she towered over him, hands on
hips. "I don't plan to sit back. I'm gonna help 'em."

Lanie looked at Dot, who was now poring over the article, for support. "Dot, you don't want to see Bliss turn into
another Kerbyville, do you?" Their neighboring county's
rapid growth had exceeded its ability to supply water. And
traffic regularly congested the main travel arteries.

"No, but if we plan carefully, we can prevent that from
happening here." She handed Lanie a salad and settled
down to eat her own lunch. "If you feel so strongly about
it, why don't you go to the Board of Supervisors' meeting
next week? Tell them what you think."

"Lots of luck," Reece said with finality. "The wheels are
already in motion."

"Not if I can help it."

Dot seemed to enjoy the tension that filled the tiny office. A slow smile spread across her lips. "Elaine might just
be the one to chock those wheels, Maurice. You may have
met your match."

As his gaze snared hers, Lanie knew what he must be thinking. That she was not equal to the challenge before her. That there was no way she could tangle with this country boy—and win. His brown eyes dared her to argue.

"It'll be a cold day in July," he said at last.

It was almost bedtime when Lanie remembered Reece's T-shirt. She found her slippers under the sofa and headed outside to the remains of the pool. As usual, Winnie tagged at her heels. Dressed only in an oversize nightshirt, Lanie hugged herself against the unseasonably cool night air and grinned when she recalled his words from earlier that day. By the time she found the pool in the dark, her slippers were soaked from puddles left by an afternoon thunderstorm.

Lanie freed Reece's sodden garment from the hole in the pool. She wrung out the water and felt a slight tug. In the next instant, the shirt was gone.

"Winnie, you come back here!" Like a flash, the horse squeezed through a gap in the fence rails. Lanie climbed over and took off after her.

"Come back, you little—"

A light flashed on in Reece's bedroom. The glare from the window fell in a long rectangle on the grass in front of Lanie. Though safely cloistered at the edge of darkness, she dared not move. Reece already thought of her as a dingbat. She didn't want to explain why she was traipsing through his yard in her nightshirt at ten o'clock.

As she watched, Reece walked to the window, cupping one hand between his eyebrows and the pane. Lord Almighty! The only two things between her eyes and his endowment were a window and a small scrap of towel held up by his free hand. Lanie bit her lip and winced at the tenderness caused by her episode with Winnie earlier in the day.

Reece shifted and appeared to look directly at her. She made like a tree, hoping he was blinded by the light in his room.

He turned and walked away from the window. One thigh peeked enticingly through the gap in his towel. Lanie's breath caught in her throat. She quickly averted her gaze. In the next moment the light flicked off.

Something cold and wet grazed her ankle, and Winnie's whiskers tickled Lanie's knee. "Gotcha!" She tried to pry the shirt from the animal's mouth, but Winnie clamped down harder for a game of tug-of-war. "Okay, if that's the way you want it . . ." She lifted the little beast and shinnied over the fence.

While Reece's shirt soaked in the bathroom sink, Lanie tweezed splinters from the back of her thighs. That horse was getting too big to be hauled over fences. Lanie winced as she removed another sliver. Her neck ached from craning to see the elusive specks. Maybe they'd eventually work their way out.

She abandoned her futile efforts and turned her attention to Reece's shirt. *If You're Not Hungry, Thank A Farmer.* As she sudsed and rinsed the garment, she thought of what Dot had said about Reece insisting on discount prices for farmers. He was obviously a caring and sensitive man. Why, then, did he want this highway splitting through the county? Surely he knew some of his farmer friends would be displaced to make way for the road.

Lanie hung the shirt over her shower rod to dry and went to the living room to find the phone book. Winnie lay curled in the recliner, watching the images on television.

"Five months old, and you're already a couch potato." Lanie flopped on the sofa with the thin local phone directory. "Let's see. County Administration Office." She jotted down the number and flipped the pages. The state highway department and several other numbers joined her list. "Tomorrow," she told Winnie, "we take action."

In the morning, Lanie ironed Reece's T-shirt, hoping to counter the effects of last night's tug-of-war. *There,* she thought, *that looks much fresher.* She eased a pair of slacks over her punctured thighs, shoved her phone list into her purse, and rounded up Winnie. After her pet's initial run-in with the gray cat, the animal behaved admirably at the store. Lanie felt certain Winnie would easily settle into the work routine. And this way, Lanie wouldn't have to leave her at home alone.

But Winnie had other ideas. The moment the door at Masardi's opened, she caught sight of the feline fluffball purring around a customer's legs. The woman's young son squatted on the floor to pet the cat. Winnie fired after the cat like a bullet out of a gun.

"Look out!" cried Lanie.

The woman grabbed up her child and tried to step out of the horse's path. Winnie, taking the straightest course to her target, darted between the customer's legs. The child giggled in glee. "Doggy! Doggy!"

Winnie rounded the corner in hot pursuit, her hooves spinning like snowbound tires. The cat, now perched atop a display shelf, watched the fun from his vantage point. Winnie ran past him and circled back around to the mother and child.

Lanie dashed to intercept her. A rope lariat snaked out and circled Winnie's neck. The horse's frantic flight abruptly halted, she hung her head and snorted twice.

"Heh, heh. I've still got the touch." Reece handed Lanie his end of the lasso, and his manner abruptly changed. "Keep your horse under control, okay?"

After the excitement had died down, Lanie approached Reece at the loading dock. He'd just helped unload a shipment of mulch. The morning sun beat down on his golden-brown skin, raising a bead of perspiration on his brow. He signed the bill of lading and handed the clipboard back to the driver. Then he retrieved a handkerchief from his hip pocket and wiped his face before acknowledging Lanie's presence.

"What'd your midget mule do now?"

"N-nothing." Why did she get so flustered when he looked at her that way? Squinting in the late-morning sunshine, his eyes appeared hooded, like a hawk's. That must be it. When he fierced his eyes like that, she felt like the prey. "She's an Arabian," she said inanely.

"What?"

"Winnie's not a mule. She's a miniaturized Arabian horse."

"Oh." Reece folded his arms across his chest, waiting for her to get to the point.

Lanie decided to forgo the battle armor and try for a gentler approach. "I'm sorry about the commotion my horse caused. I'll hold her tighter next time." She rubbed at a mosquito bite on her arm.

"C'mon, let's get out of this hot sun." He touched her arm as they stepped inside.

Instead of cooling off, Lanie suddenly felt twenty degrees warmer. As Reece reached up to pull the sliding metal door down its track, she couldn't help noticing the sinewy strength in his body. Lanie tried to wipe the lust off her face and replace it with a look of polished professionalism. He already thought she was a fruitcake. She didn't want to make matters worse by making him think she was a seductive fruitcake.

He walked beside her as they passed between rows of green plastic flowerpots. "What I don't understand is, why would anyone buy a nonworking animal? And why did you name the thing Winnie?"

"What did you expect me to name her...Flicka?" She grinned as he considered it.

"That's a start." Reece reached out to straighten a display on Lanie's side of the aisle. His arm brushed her body. She shivered at his touch, remembering the sight of him wrapped only in a towel.

His eyes caught hers. He must have felt the spark, too.

"Cats catch mice, dogs hunt..." Reece continued, resuming his stride as if nothing had passed between them. "Cows give milk, and you can ride a normal horse. Why did you waste your money on a shrimp like Winnie?"

"She was a gift of love. And I don't consider his money wasted."

Reece arched one eyebrow. His silence invited her to say more. Around Reece, Lanie found herself shy and vulnerable. If she talked about her father now, she might cry. They approached the office together, and Reece stepped back to let her enter first.

"Oh, I almost forgot," said Lanie. "Here's your T-shirt. I washed and pressed it for you."

Howard popped his head in the door behind him, but Reece appeared not to notice.

"I was wondering what happened to my favorite shirt. Forgot I left it at your house." Lanie tried to stop him before he said more, but he took the shirt and held it up. "Ironed, huh? Never wore an ironed T-shirt before, but there's always a first." Lanie hadn't heard him talk this much before.

She tried to shut him up. "Umm, Reece—"

"You don't iron your nighties, do you?" Reece grinned broadly and plunged farther into the mire. "You know, like the oversized pajama top you wore last night?"

Behind them, Howard cleared his throat.

Reece whirled around and started at the sight of his employee.

"Uh, I'll come back later," said Howard, "when you're not so busy." He turned to leave, but Reece stopped him with a hand on the shoulder.

"Don't go. It's not, ah, what you think."

"I don't think nothin'." Howard shot a glance at Lanie who stood openmouthed at Reece's unexpected teasing. "But if I was to think something," he winked at Reece, "I'd think you know how to pick 'em. Anyhow, it's about time."

For the moment, Reece seemed at a loss for words. "Howard..."

"I just stopped by to ask y'all if you want one of Etta's burgers. But being as you're so busy, I'll just make myself scarce." Howard left as quickly as he'd entered.

Reece folded the shirt. He stepped to the door and shoved it shut with his heel. "I'm sorry. I didn't know he was standing there." Then, as if unaware of what he was doing, he crumpled the shirt in his hands.

Lanie fumbled with a pencil on the desk. "It's nothing new. I'm used to fighting my reputation." At the shocked expression on his face, she hastened to add, "A lot of people think I'm strange because I have a unique pet and weird things happen to me. Like last night—"

"Yes, about last night." Reece leaned against the closed door and toyed with the design on the shirt. "I have to warn you, the law's hell on Peeping Toms around here." One corner of his mouth lifted in a crooked smile. "Next time you want to peep, just let me know. You don't have to sneak around outside my bedroom window for a free show."

"I didn't . . . I wasn't . . ." The audacity of this guy! "For your information, Maurice Masardi, I've seen little boys before, so your generous offer is quite unnecessary."

Reece laughed at the uncomplimentary comparison. He didn't know what had prompted him to tease Lanie as he had, but he knew he deserved the insult. Lanie stared back at him, still breathing fire. One hand rested in a challenging manner on her hip. Even in slacks, she looked sexy. Irrationally he found himself wanting to hold her and kiss away her anger. He wanted her rigid stance to melt away as he took her into his arms. *Easy, Masardi,* he cautioned himself, *this is your employee.*

He met her gaze and noticed the defiant, upward thrust of her chin. But the eyes told the true story. In them he read a challenge, but there was something more subtle, as well. Fear, perhaps?

Automatically he took a step toward Lanie. She retreated a half step, stopping with a grimace when the backs of her legs touched the desk. Reece's eyes trailed to the grim line of her mouth. A faint blue spot marked the left corner of her lip. One more step, and he reached out to touch the bruise. By now, the hardness had left her eyes and was replaced with curiosity. Her expression softened and her eyes widened slightly, all of which made him want to touch more than her lip. Lightly he ran the pad of his thumb over the tender flesh. He had forgotten how soft a woman's lips could be.

Involuntarily his tongue flicked out to moisten his own lips. Lanie innocently repeated the gesture. The wet, pink tip touched his thumb, and Reece self-consciously returned his hand to his side.

What had gotten into him? He didn't need to get involved with a woman, especially this one who seemed to turn everything she touched into disaster. And although he begrudgingly acknowledged the attraction she held for him, he knew a fling was out of the question. Partly because she didn't seem to be the "fling" type, but mostly because succumbing to his baser urges would mess up their working relationship. Why, when things were starting to look up, did she have to bungle into his life and complicate it?

Reece wiped his damp palms on his back pockets. "You, ah, should have put ice on that lip right after you hurt it." God, what an idiot! Of course she knew that.

A shy smile that seemed awkward on her face lifted the bruise a fraction. In an instant it was gone, replaced by a look of pure devilment. "Thank you, Dr. Masardi," she said, easing herself away from the desk. "What do you recommend for splinters?"

Reece squinted at her in consternation. What did that have to do with her bruised lip. "Huh?"

"My sit-down is full of fence splinters. Since it was your fence that caused it, the least you can do is recommend somebody to pull them out." Her lower lip pouted out, but he could see she was trying not to laugh. "What do y'all have around here...midwives?"

The little fox! She was enjoying this far too much. Reece walked over to his desk and laid the shirt on one corner, placing his truck keys on top. The action put some distance between them and gave him a moment to respond without sounding winded. He sat on the desktop and rested his feet on the chair. He smiled at her reaction to his uncharacteristic impropriety.

"Nope," he said, "I don't know of any midwives around here. But I can give you the name of a good veterinarian."

Reece was immediately rewarded with the smile Lanie could no longer hold back. For some reason, it warmed him.

"I doubt that an animal doctor could help me."

"On the contrary. This one is an expert in your problem." At Lanie's quizzical expression, he continued. "His sign says 'Specializes in Horses, Cattle, and Asses.' What more could you want?"

To his amazement, she laughed out loud. It was a pleasant, musical sound. He had half expected her to react with embarrassment, or to try to cover her surprise. What he hadn't expected was for her to laugh at herself so wholeheartedly.

She slid into her chair, wincing slightly. "I deserved that. Touché."

"Don't you mean, 'tushy'?"

She groaned, and Reece held up his hands as if to fend off thrown objects. His watch beeped twice to announce the noon hour.

"Look, Howard ought to be back soon. Do you want to get a burger from Etta's?" He could have kicked himself as he watched her waver in indecision. *Fool!* he told himself. *What about not getting involved with an employee? Especially this one!* Mentally he reassured himself that this was nothing more than if he were sharing lunch with Violet or Howard. But he knew better.

"Thanks, but if you don't mind, I need to spend my lunchtime making phone calls." She retrieved a scrap of paper from her designer purse. "However, if you don't want me to conduct my 'Stop the Highway' campaign from here, I'll understand."

Reece stood and shoved the chair under the desk. Of course he minded. If that look on her face was any indication, she was determined to wreck his plan for the business. What had he done to deserve this kind of punishment? Since she wasn't paid for her lunchtime, she was entitled to use it as she pleased. And even if he tried to stop her, Reece had no doubt she'd redouble her efforts to foul up the highway plan. He clenched his teeth in frustration.

"Do whatever the hell you want," he muttered and stalked out of the room.

Chapter Three

By Friday, Lanie had joined a committee to oppose construction of the highway. Her initial assignment, distributing the group's fliers, should be simple enough, she reasoned. All she had to do was ask Violet to tuck one into each shopper's bag.

As for Reece, ever since Lanie had mentioned fighting the proposed highway, his demeanor had been businesslike and remote. She tapped her pencil against the typewriter. Maybe she shouldn't have said anything to him about her efforts.

Touching a finger to her lip, she recalled the gentleness with which he'd touched her and the concern that had been evident in his soul-searching eyes. She recalled the way he'd smiled as he joked with her. Then, just when she was beginning to think he had a personality, he had turned into Mr. Businessman.

Reece's deep voice came to her from outside the office. "Mom, where've you been the past couple of days? We've missed you."

"Why? Does Elaine need my help?"

Reece hesitated and cleared his throat. "No, she's doing fine." Lanie breathed a sigh of relief. "Next week I'll take her with me on some deliveries."

Lanie looked at the stacks of forms on her desk and wondered how he could consider having her gallivant around the countryside with all these papers still a mess. Besides, she had no desire to share the close confines of a pickup truck cab with her stone-faced boss. Or worse, what if a drive in the country put him in a good mood and he turned on the charm she'd glimpsed Tuesday? She wouldn't be able to deal with it.

Lanie grew annoyed with herself for having eavesdropped on their conversation in the first place. She went to the filing cabinet and started arranging the vaccine order forms in their rightful places. Even so, Dot's voice drifted to her above the rattling of papers.

"Oh, honey, I've been having the best time. It's amazing how a person can live in one area for sixty years and never visit the local museums and historical sites." Her soft voice fairly bubbled with excitement. "My friend and I have been setting out to rectify the situation."

Reece's laugh was one of amusement. "Great. I'm glad you're having a good time. While you're in town, why don't you pick up a party dress for the Bliss Banquet? And let me know what color it is so I can buy you a corsage to match."

There was a brief silence. When she spoke, her words were calculated. "Thank you, honey, but that won't be necessary. I already have someone to accompany me."

Reece's voice was soft, almost hurt sounding. "You didn't have to find an escort. I'd have been honored to take you again."

Again, Dot seemed to struggle for just the right words. "That's very sweet, but Walter isn't an escort, he's my date."

The quiet that followed magnified every click of Lanie's heels as she crossed the room to retrieve the seed catalog. She debated whether to close the door to help shut out their conversation. No, she decided, that might seem too obvious.

"I see." Lanie could tell by his tone that he didn't.

"If you need a date, dear, why don't you ask Elaine?"

Lanie somersaulted the catalog across her desk. On impact, the phone skidded over the edge and clanged to the floor.

Great, she thought, *Zany Lanie strikes again.* She stooped to pick up the phone and was reeling in the receiver when two pairs of shoes appeared in the office.

"Elaine, dear, are you okay?"

"Y-yes, ma'am, just a bit klutzy today." She stood and set the phone back in its rightful place on her desk.

"What's today got to do with it?" Reece glared at her. Lanie glared back.

Dot laid a hand on her son's arm. "Now, Maurice, you promised you'd be nice to Elaine." Dot hitched her purse strap up on her shoulder and sidled toward the door. "You have something to ask Elaine, so I'll make myself scarce. Bye!"

Dot closed the door behind her, leaving Lanie to deal with Reece and his scowl. She could tell he wasn't looking forward to asking her to accompany him to the banquet. Well, that made two of them! She had to let him off the hook.

"Look, you don't have to—"

"You're damn right I don't have to. What I do want to ask you is to put some shoes on your horse if you insist on bringing her here."

"Huh?"

"Every day your horse gets the rips and starts chasing my cat through the store. This morning she lost her footing and crashed into one of the display bins." He reached past her for the telephone directory and flipped to the listings for Bliss County.

The nearness of him was intoxicating. If there'd been room, Lanie would have retreated. This was one of those times when she was overwhelmed by his forcefulness. With his elbow mere inches from her own, she hoped he wouldn't notice her losing battle with her emotions. Part of her was relieved that he hadn't asked her to the banquet. Part was miffed that he'd been so short with her. But mostly she was hurt that he didn't want her to go with him, that he chose instead to chastise her for her horse's behavior. She wondered if he'd make her pay for the damaged bin.

It's just as well, she soothed herself. *We're as different as night and day. Silly and sober.*

He handed her the phone book. Their hands touched briefly. Lanie had never before been so aware of an accidental touch. Unreasonably, she wished it had been intentional. She looked up at Reece and saw that the angry glare was gone. From this close range, she could see the tiny untanned creases that gathered at the outer edges of his eyes.

Reece pointed to the name he'd circled. "This guy is the best farrier in Bliss."

"Thanks. I'll give him a call."

Reece stayed where he was, looking for all the world like there was something else he wanted to say. He absentmindedly scratched his flat stomach, and Lanie wished he hadn't drawn her attention to the superb fit of his cotton shirt. Even though he wore shorts every day, his shirt was always neatly tucked into the narrow waistband. Lanie forced her eyes away from his waistband, fearing her imagination might delve lower.

"There is one other thing I need to ask you," he ventured. Panic filled Lanie's chest, squeezing her lungs until she could hardly breathe. He was going to ask her to the banquet after all! Her conflicting feelings confused her. How should she answer him?

"Yes," she said, her breath coming out in a gush.

Reece reached into his front shorts pocket. So much for reining in her imagination. He extracted a crumpled piece of paper that gave no hint of an attempt to fold it. He smoothed it out and handed it to her. "About this flier of yours urging 'all interested persons' to attend next week's Board of Supervisors' meeting." He was smiling, but Lanie detected a muscle twitching in his jaw. "I'd be most happy to accept your kind invitation."

Lanie didn't like the dangerous gentleness of his tone.

"And while we're on the subject, next time you want to distribute letters to our customers . . . don't."

"What's the matter, Reece, afraid I might convince your farmer friends that the highway is not in their best interest?"

Reece snorted as he turned around and reached for the doorknob. "The farmers don't need an outsider to tell them what's in their best interest."

"Maybe that's what you think, but there are lots of others who share my views. I'll spend every spare minute this weekend distributing fliers and drumming up supporters. Don't be surprised if this highway lunacy is defeated next week."

Reece paused half in and half out of the door. "Gee," he said, a grin tugging at the corner of his mouth, "and I would have thought that a woman as pretty as you would have much better ways to spend her weekends."

He closed the door behind him as he exited. A second later, it opened again and Reece stuck his head in.

"By the way, your horoscope this morning said not to underestimate a powerful opponent."

Lanie stared after him. When had he started reading *her* horoscope?

Lanie pushed an annoying strand of hair behind her ear and pried at the stained rubber appliqué adorning the bottom of the bathtub. "Powerful opponent, indeed," she muttered as she thought of Reece's comment earlier that day. "I'll bet he's not half as powerful as the glue on the bottom of this."

After taking Winnie to get fitted for shoes and making a trip to the local merchants to post her fliers, she'd decided to attack the mildew in the tiny bathroom.

By the time she finished, the old tub almost shone. Lanie was feeling smug when she heard a knock at the back door. She entered the kitchen and found Reece peering in at her through the glass portion of the door. Wondering what was important enough to bring him to her house, Lanie reached for the knob.

"Hello, neighbor," she said as he wiped his feet on the mat and stepped inside.

Reece flashed an embarrassed grin and stuffed his hands into his pockets. "You got any iced tea? It's as hot as blazes outside."

Didn't he have iced tea at home? Never mind, she'd be hospitable. "Sure," she said, opening the refrigerator. "Do you want lemon?"

"No thanks, just sugar." Reece paced the kitchen while she got a glass and poured the tea. "The place looks nice. You've even got stuff on the walls already." He reached up and toyed with the decorative kitchen witch that dangled over the sink.

"Thanks. If my house is disorganized, my mind feels cluttered. So I try not to take any chances." She handed him the glass and watched him take a swallow of the cool liquid. "Won't you come sit down?" she asked, gesturing toward the living room. "Excluding Dot, you're my first visitor."

Their bodies collided in the doorway. Lanie jerked away from the pleasant feel of his hard-muscled arm. The last time they'd accidentally touched, the memory of it had distracted her from her work. Better to avoid it in the first place and save herself some agony. "I, uh, forgot how small this house is. You go first."

Lanie followed him into the living room and plunked down in the chair that catty-cornered his. She tried not to wince when the backs of her splintery legs touched the rough upholstery fabric.

"My house is just like this one, only in reverse."

Lanie wondered why, as part owner of such a successful store, he didn't own a bigger house.

Reece downed the rest of his tea and continued. "Both were built as housing for my great-great-grandfather's grown children so they'd help him work the farm. After my father lost money several years in a row, he sold off some of the land and this house and opened the feed store." He traced a pattern in the moisture on the glass. "When I graduated from college, I bought the one next door, partly to keep it in the family and partly to stay close to my parents in case they needed me."

Lanie leaned back in her chair and propped her bare feet on the coffee table. Ah, much better!

Winnie trotted into the room and jumped onto the sofa beside Reece. The little horse butted him in the chest in an attempt to get him to play with her. "You ought to break her of this," said Reece. "When she grows up, she could hurt somebody." He rubbed her chin anyway.

"I'm told she'll weigh less than two hundred pounds when she's fully grown," Lanie defended. "Besides, she's gentle with children. She seems to know they're more fragile than adults."

"Yeah, I've been meaning to say something about that."

So now the reason for this unexpected visit was coming out.

"The feed store has been overrun with kids these past few days."

"Word must have gotten out about Winnie. She seems to have that effect on people."

"Yeah, well, they're driving me crazy."

"Violet tells me sales are up this week. Maybe you should beef up your pet center with toys and a bigger variety of food. And you could even sell some horse books and plastic toy horses as souvenirs for the kids. May as well take advantage of a good thing."

Reece rubbed the stubble along his jaw. "You've got a good point there. Would you see that those items are ordered on Monday?"

"Sure."

He allowed Winnie to lie on his lap. He idly patted her fuzzy ribs. "There's one other thing. Do you have a pair of binoculars I can borrow?"

The binoculars from her dad's fishing boat—where had she put them? Oh, yes, the closet. "Sure do. I'll get them for you." She rose and rubbed the smarting skin on the back of her legs. In a minute she was back with the binoculars.

"Thanks," said Reece as he accepted them. He flashed her an awkward smile. "I, uh, have been noticing a strange car at my mother's house. Just thought I'd keep an eye on her.''

"Spying, huh?" Lanie walked over to the window and pulled back the curtain. "With that kind of attitude, you'll never make friends with Walter."

Even though the air conditioner was running, his face turned red-hot. He shook the binoculars at her. "With all the weirdos running around nowadays, you can never be too cautious."

Lanie knew better than to push the subject, but she couldn't help asking, "Don't you think it'd be easier to check him out from up close than by spying on him from across the street?" She touched her forehead. "I know! You could invite them both over for dinner!"

Reece eased Winnie off his lap. Standing, he handed Lanie the binoculars. "Fine. When do you want us?"

Lanie almost dropped the glasses. "B-but, I meant . . .'' How did she get herself into these messes?

"I like almost anything but casseroles. If you want me to bring something, just let me know."

"Uh, gee, thanks."

"No, thank *you.*''

"Excuse me, but I think I need a cold drink. Do you want a refill?" He didn't, so she went to the kitchen to get the tea and gather her wits. What she needed was the stronger, Northern version of this beverage . . . a Long Island iced tea.

When she returned, he stared fixedly at her. "You didn't get all those splinters out, did you?"

"I've been busy."

"That fence is made out of salt-treated wood. If you don't get the splinters out soon, you'll get a bad infection."

He seemed more angry than concerned, but Lanie refused to let him rattle her nerves. "Too late, they're already infected. But don't worry, I've been taking hot baths to try to soak them out.''

The sound that came out of Reece was clearly exasperation. He brushed past her and headed for the bathroom. Rather than close the door, he started rummaging through the medicine cabinet. ''Where are your tweezers?''

''It's no use. I've already tried that.''

''But *I* haven't.'' He found a package of cotton balls and a bottle of peroxide and set them on the toilet.

''Look, you don't need to—''

''The tweezers. Where are they?'' By now he was piling things in her sink.

She squeezed into the bathroom and gently pushed him aside. She wished she could touch him without noticing the crispness of the blond hairs on his arms and the sinewy strength of his muscles. ''I had all this stuff in order, and now you're messing it up,'' she griped. ''Here are the damn tweezers—pardon me.''

For some reason, Reece seemed to think that was funny. He tucked the peroxide and cotton balls under one arm and took her by the elbow. When she realized he was heading toward her bedroom, she dug her heels in. ''You're not getting any strange ideas, are you?''

''Do you want me to?''

''Maybe I should call Dot and ask her to do it.''

''I've vaccinated cattle and gelded horses. Trust me, I can pull a couple of splinters out of your butt.''

He switched on the overhead light, and mounds of ruffles and lace greeted them. Reece looked slowly around the room.

''You like pink, don't you?''

''It's mauve.''

''It figures.''

"Daddy called me his 'rose among the thorns.' The curtains and bedspread were his sweet-sixteen gift to me. He liked for me to have girlish things." Even at sixteen, she'd thought the flowing folds of fabric were a bit much, but it irked her to think that Reece was mocking her father's gift.

He went to the nightstand and switched on the lamp. "May as well get this over with." Reece turned to her and held the tweezers clawlike. "Drop your drawers."

"Sorry to disappoint you, but the splinters are in my thighs. The shorts stay on."

An exaggerated look of disappointment crossed his handsome face and was quickly replaced by a teasing grin. Lanie couldn't help returning a smile. "You're not supposed to be enjoying this." She sprawled facedown on the bed and reached into the nightstand drawer for a flashlight. "Here, you might need this."

Reece knelt at the side of the bed. "I'll try to be quick about it," he said, his voice now as gentle and somber as a physician's.

Lanie pressed her face into the pillow and tried to block out the feel of his callused fingers against her smarting thighs. He sponged peroxide over the stinging wounds. When he rested an elbow familiarly on her bottom, she felt a burning sensation in the pit of her stomach.

He's not your type. He's not your type. Lanie mentally chanted the words. He'd make somebody a good husband one day, but it wouldn't be her. *Couldn't* be her. And he'd be a good father, too. He was strong, yet gentle. He'd make a wonderful role model for a son. She gritted her teeth. Unfortunately, good mothers were not made from people with nicknames like Zany Lanie.

Reece swore softly. Lanie moved the pillow over her head to blot out the male huskiness of his voice.

"What's the matter—that hurt?"

"Mmrrmph."

"Hold on a minute. I can't get at the *seat* of the problem from this angle." In the next moment he was straddling her, backward. He must have slipped his shoes off, for now his toes lightly grazed the sides of her breasts.

Lanie inhaled suddenly and got a noseful of pillowcase. She tried to throw the pillow off her head, but Reece was firmly planted in the middle of her back. A claustrophobic panic took over, and she moved to get up. Something sharp pricked her thigh.

"Ow!"

"What the—"

"Get off me, you big oaf."

He rolled off and lay on the bed beside her. One end of the pillow came up. Lanie was surprised to find him looking in at her, his face only inches from hers. Her breath came in fast pants. She yanked the pillow off her head and sat up.

"You were suffocating me!"

Reece remained where he was, leaning on one elbow and looking a lot like he should be posing for an underwear commercial. "You were the one who put the pillow over your head."

"I was trying to block out y—the pain. That's it, the pain."

Reece looked doubtful.

"What were you doing on my back?"

He appeared amused. "Trying to get a grip on things. Did you like it?"

"Of course not," she lied.

"Why? Would you rather be on top?" Reece flopped over on his back and held out his arms in invitation.

Lanie folded her arms across her chest. She was drawn to him, there was no denying it. There was nothing she would have liked more than lying in his arms, surrendering to his caresses. But she felt, more than thought, that a physical relationship with Reece was doomed just as much as an emotional one. There was no way she could simply go to bed with him and not get emotionally involved. She sat back on her heels, putting a little extra distance between them.

Then, plastering on a broad smile for bravado, she said, "Forget it. I'll wear these splinters until I get blood poisoning. Then you'll have my backside on your conscience."

"It's already on my mind, so what's the difference?" Reece tucked his hands behind his head and allowed his eyes to roam over her.

Why the hell was he acting this way? Maybe it was just to watch her blush, he reasoned. Her fair skin glowed a becoming shade of pink in contrast to her dark hair.

No, it was more than that. For the past three years he'd been in strict control of his life, even to the point of avoiding casual dates. Why risk upsetting the rigid life he'd made for himself? When his father had first started showing signs of senility, Reece had become the model of reliability. By now, it had become out of character for him to joke around and tease an employee, especially one as feminine and beautiful as Lanie. But even if there were room for a woman in his five-year plan, Lanie wouldn't be the one. Maybe in a few years, when he could devote more time to a relationship, he'd settle down with a nice, stable woman, one who'd offer no surprises.

So why did he find himself lying in Lanie's bed, inviting her into his arms and so much as confessing that he'd noticed the wiggle in her walk? He had no idea, and he quickly became annoyed with himself for letting her bother him.

"Well, don't just sit there, let's finish getting those splinters out," he said more brusquely than he'd intended. At her hurt expression he immediately regretted being so sharp with her. It wasn't her fault he was feeling this unwanted attraction. She hadn't come on to him; in fact, *he* had been seducing *her*.

He knelt beside her on the bed. His voice gentler than before, he said, "There are just two or three more splinters. I should have them out in a minute." He held up one hand in a Boy Scout salute. "No monkey business. Scout's honor."

"All right, but if your fingers stray so much as one inch from my splinters, I'm reporting you to the Labor Board."

Lanie moved to her side and ground her teeth in frustration. Was the man schizophrenic? Both times he'd allowed her to glimpse his lighter side, he'd immediately afterward become solemn and unapproachable. Well, two could play this game. She resolved once again to maintain a businesslike demeanor with him. She'd have to fight her impulsive nature every step of the way, but she was determined not to become vulnerable to his charm again.

True to his word, Reece removed the remaining wood fragments in a matter of only a minute or two. When he was finished, he quickly dabbed her wounds with the foaming medicine. The action was so brief and perfunctory Lanie barely had time to notice what he'd done. In a moment he picked up the first-aid items and walked around to her side of the bed. He offered his free hand, but she ignored it.

"Thanks," she said, heading for the door before he could become charming and friendly—and appealing—again. She glanced at him as he accompanied her back to the bathroom to return the stuff to the medicine chest. Even when he turned the charm and friendliness off like a switch, the appeal was still there. Maybe, Lanie rationalized as they walked to the living room together, Reece would be the perfect subject on which to practice being nonspontaneous. If she could pass that test, she knew, she'd be a changed woman.

He was picking up his tea glass, but Lanie stopped him. "Don't worry about that. I'll get it later." She stood facing him, her hands clasped primly behind her back. "Thank you for your help. I feel better already."

"My pleasure," said Reece. Then he grinned. "Sorry I stabbed you with the tweezers."

Oh, no, thought Lanie. *He's doing it again. He's turning into Mr. Wonderful.* The heavy-lidded look he gave her belonged in the bedroom. How was she supposed to keep that promise she'd made to herself when he was standing within touching distance in glorious tan-and-muscle 3-D? She could feel her resolve weakening.

It crumpled a second later when he reached up to move a wayward strand of her hair to its rightful place. When his hands touched her shoulders, she reflexively reached up as if to ward him off. Her grip settled on his wrists. Instead of pushing him away, her fingers lay lightly on his forearms as his big hands caressed her shoulders. Her mouth suddenly dry, Lanie licked her lips. She heard loud breathing, but she wasn't sure whether it was Reece's or her own.

She gazed up into his warm brown eyes, their gentleness reminding her of tame deer she'd seen in the nature center at Maymont Park. However, this was no tame deer, she realized. Reece was more like a wild stag—strong, with a hint of underlying danger. The distance between them slowly closed as Reece lowered his head to her. His words, barely a whisper, broke the thick silence that had settled around them.

"I suppose," he said, his gaze intent upon her lips, "it would be improper for an employer to kiss his office manager."

"Yes," said Lanie, her eyes traveling to the firm softness of his mouth, "and it would be improper for the office manager to kiss him back."

Everything around them seemed to evaporate when he kissed her. There was no time, no place, no broken vow...nothing but the moist warmth of his mouth on hers. The heat traveled through her entire body, and Lanie was barely aware when her hands slid along his arms and down to his trim waist. In her daze, she welcomed the crushing presence of his solid chest against her breasts as he took her closer into the circle of his arms.

He tasted sweet, like sugared tea. His lips tickled where they whisked her face as he dropped little kisses across her cheek and nuzzled the tender spot below her ear. As in a dance with no steps, they improvised, making up the movements in time to a rapidly increasing tempo.

The imaginary music crescendoed and gave way to a gently wafting melody that seemed to linger between them even as they stepped apart.

Her mind cloudy with desire, Lanie could do no more than stare back at the brown eyes that gleamed like dark chocolate.

Bittersweet chocolate.

Chapter Four

Lanie lay back in the tub and jiggled the chain with her toe. They sure didn't make bathtubs like these anymore. She had filled the old clawfooted monster until the water grazed her chin. The hot soak helped ease the stinging in her thighs, but Lanie knew a cold shower would have done more to calm her libido.

Why was it that every time Reece came near her, she turned into a stark-raving idiot? True, she wasn't normally as steady as a rock, but the man completely unnerved her! One minute she was vowing to maintain a polite, business-like relationship with her employer, and the next she was in his arms, kissing him for all she was worth.

It wasn't the first time she'd been kissed, but remembering this one made her feel as giddy as a schoolgirl. She recalled the look on Reece's face after they'd kissed. Shock, pure and simple. As if she'd slapped him. Then he'd mumbled an apology and left her standing there, gaping after him as he'd let himself out. Men could be such jerks sometimes.

No, *she* was the jerk. The last thing Reece needed was a dingbat such as herself to mess up his calm and orderly life. The man was obviously family material. He didn't strike her as the type to dally with a woman and then go his merry way. So, why then, did he kiss and run?

Maybe her weirdness was rubbing off on him.

Lanie groaned and sank deeper into the bubbles. All her life she'd hoped she would outgrow her wackiness, and now she was bringing others down with her. She rinsed off and stepped out of the tub. She briskly toweled herself dry, but she couldn't rub away the memory of Reece's gentle touch.

After donning a red cotton nightshirt, she made a quick check to see that the doors were locked. The binoculars lay on the coffee table where she'd left them earlier. Lanie picked them up and took them to her bedroom to put them away.

Winnie was sprawled across the double bed. Little horsey snores could be heard above the crickets' chirping. With the binoculars still in her hand, Lanie moved to the window to close the blinds when a movement in Reece's room caught her eye. Impulsively she lifted the glasses to her eyes.

He was taking off his shirt! With a pang, she remembered the hard feel of his chest when he'd held her in his arms to kiss her. Lanie adjusted the focus and took in the dark blond curls that circled his nipples and tapered down into his corduroy shorts. His hands reached for the zipper and in a second the shorts were lying in a heap on the floor. Reece stretched and lazily scratched his bare side with slow, circular motions.

Lanie lowered the glasses and wiped the fog off the eyepieces. If he took off one more article of clothing, she might be tempted to leap the fence that separated their properties and break down his front door. She picked up the phone from the nightstand and dialed Reece's number. She had to save him from herself.

His hand was already on the waistband of his briefs when his head jerked toward the table by his bed. He sat on the bed, his back to the window, and picked up the receiver.

"Hello."

Lanie's mouth flapped a couple of times, but nothing came out. *How do you tell your boss you're drooling over his body?*

"Hello! Who is this?"

"Um, hi." Then it took over. The imp that had plagued her all her life now possessed her, and Lanie's lips turned up in wicked amusement. "Could you stand closer to the window? I can't see the good stuff."

Reece darted a glance over his shoulder. Without a word, he stood and walked to the window.

Lanie couldn't believe her eyes. He was actually doing it! She raised the glasses and peered through them, ostensibly to read the expression on his face, but she couldn't help letting her gaze wander from his crooked smile to his muscle-rounded shoulders, well-defined pectorals, and washboard stomach. She couldn't stand here and peep at him like some pervert. She was about to lower the binoculars for the last time when Reece reached up and pulled the shade. His silhouette bent and removed the one remaining garment.

Good grief. That shadowy movement probably did more to fuel her wayward thoughts than if she'd actually seen him take off his briefs. Lanie replaced the receiver on the hook and gave a second thought to a nice, cold shower.

If Reece had seemed sexy and desirable Friday night, that image was now replaced with one of grim determination...and maybe a little bit of smugness.

Lanie folded her hands in her lap and looked around the public meeting room at the elbow-to-elbow crowd. Well, she could be smug, too. The turnout wouldn't have been anywhere near as large if she hadn't enlisted other highway opponents to help call more than half the homes in Bliss. If bodies counted for anything, then her side would win hands down.

Reece was talking animatedly with a representative from the highway department. He watched while the other man traced a finger along the large stand-up map display. Reece nodded a couple of times, looking as serious as if the whole decision rested on his shoulders alone.

The chairman of the Board of Supervisors went to his seat on the raised platform at the front of the room and tapped the microphone. Those still standing quickly took their seats on the hard, wooden benches.

After more than a week of passing out fliers, telephoning strangers and debating the highway issue with anyone who would listen, Lanie was glad it would soon be decided. She fumbled in her purse for her lucky rock and rubbed the polished surface between her thumb and the crook of her forefinger. *Rock, don't fail me now.*

The other board members settled into their seats, and the floor opened for discussion of a proposed dirt-bike raceway at the outer edge of the county.

That matter quickly disposed of, the podium was turned over to the highway representative. He droned on for a while about the cost, on ramps and exits, and the number of families who'd be displaced.

Occasionally Lanie found that her eyes strayed to Reece, who sat erect and alert at the front of the room. In contrast to the graying and balding men on either side and behind him, his hair shone goldish yellow under the artificial lights. Like his seatmates, Reece wore a coat and tie. About halfway into the presentation, he removed his navy blazer and tugged at his shirt collar. Lanie almost expected him to un-button his cuffs and roll up the white sleeves. It would have seemed more natural than the way he looked now, biceps and broad shoulders straining at the cotton fabric. Lanie pulled her eyes away from the sight and worried the rock some more.

"Fine," said the chairman once the presentation was fin-ished. "Then, if no one has any further discussion, we'll table the matter until next month's meeting. By then we should have a more definite figure on the cost."

What? Table the matter? Lanie jumped to her feet. "Wait a minute! I have a question. What about the vote?"

"Please identify yourself."

Lanie grew uncomfortably warm under the scrutiny of all those pairs of eyes. But now was not the time to let a little stage fright hold her back. She took a deep breath.

"Elaine Weatherford. I live in the Hancock District. What I want to know is, what happened to the vote that was supposed to be taken tonight?"

Chairman Morrison rammed a finger into his hairy ear and twirled it. "What vote?" He turned to the man beside him. "We didn't advertise a vote, did we, Harley?"

Harley said no, and then Reece stood up. "Reece Ma-sardi, Hancock District. To my knowledge, Mr. Morrison, head counts are irrelevant in matters like this. In the past, the Board of Supervisors has required signed petitions from a percentage of registered voters in Bliss."

He turned so that he could address the rest of the assem-bly as well. His gaze briefly caught Lanie's.

"In order to save time," he continued, "I move that we authorize an environmental impact study to begin immedi-ately."

A woman at the back of the room said, "Seconded."

Lanie felt like throwing her rock at him. "He can't move while I still have the floor!"

"Anybody disagree with Mr. Masardi's suggestion?" said Mr. Morrison.

Still standing, Lanie shot her hand up. "I do." A scattering of others raised their hands.

"All in favor?"

Half the people in the room responded with a show of hands. It was a far cry more than had opposed it. What had happened to all her supporters?

"So passed."

"That's not fair! I had the floor!"

Evelyn, the woman sitting beside her, pulled Lanie's sleeve until she sat back down. "We do things kind of casually around here," she whispered. "But don't you worry none about that study. It'll take months for them to finish it, so we'll have plenty of time to get those petitions signed."

Lanie was so angry she could have spit nails. She wanted to lash out at someone, but Evelyn didn't deserve her wrath. Evelyn had spent many hours on the phone and even used part of her grocery money to hire a sitter for her six kids so she could be here tonight. As folks started filing from the room, Lanie thanked the woman for her help and they discussed strategy for the next step.

After they'd said their goodbyes, Lanie took out her key ring and held it in her fist with the keys protruding between her fingers. The parking lot was well lit and her car could be seen from the road, but old habits died hard. From the looks of people standing by their cars and chatting with old friends, they could have just come from a family reunion.

Lanie had reached her car and was pushing the key into the lock when a voice behind her startled her.

"I was hoping I'd see you before—"

On reflex, Lanie jerked the keys out and spun around to face her assailant. Wielding the ignition key like a knife, she stared up into the black shadow of her intruder's face.

"—you left." He slowly ran a hand down one side of his jaw and up the other, then repeated the gesture in reverse. "I realize we're on different sides of the fence as far as the highway goes, but let's keep our fight in the public meeting room where it belongs. Okay?"

Lanie relaxed from her coiled position. With a sigh, she let the keys dangle loosely from her fingers. "I thought you were a demented attacker."

Reece laughed. "Sorry to disappoint you. I just wanted to make sure you're coming to work tomorrow."

"Tomorrow's Friday—why wouldn't I be?"

Reece turned and half sat, half leaned against the front fender of her small car. The lamp's yellow glow cast a shadow across his face, making the outline of his nose more pronounced, his hawklike eyebrows more prominent. When he leaned back and rested his hands on the hood, his blazer gaped open and the buttons on his shirt strained against the holes.

"After tonight, I wasn't sure you'd want to," he said.

"I wanted to hit you over the head with that map display. Why didn't you tell me we needed to get petitions signed?"

Even in the eerie yellow glow of the lamplight, Lanie could see his crooked smile.

"I would've if you'd asked."

She jammed the key into the lock and turned it. "How *kind* of you. Why don't you just go home and laugh about how you made a fool of me in front of all those people!"

Lanie threw her purse over to the passenger seat and slid behind the wheel. She was about to slam the door shut, but

Reece had gotten up and was holding it open. He insinuated his body between the door and the car.

Though he had embarrassed her and was now holding her and her car captive, she refused to cry in front of him. Lanie tugged again on the door, but he wouldn't budge. "Is there a reason you're harassing me?" she asked.

"Are you always so defensive?"

Lanie had to turn sideways in the bucket seat and look up to meet his gaze. He definitely had the power position here. "Look, it's late. I have to go home before Winnie trashes the house."

She could tell by the way he hesitated and squared his mouth that he was dying to say something about her keeping the horse inside. But he didn't. She gave him credit for knowing enough to keep silent about it.

"I didn't come over here to gloat about what happened tonight," he said. "I just wanted to ask how the paperwork's coming."

"The paperwork?" She'd only found out tonight that she needed to start getting signatures on the petitions. So far the only paperwork she'd done was the flier he'd fussed at her for putting in customers' sacks.

"Yeah. How's it coming with the billing and ordering? You know . . . paperwork."

"Oh, *that* paperwork." How did this man have the power to rattle her cage so? "Between Dot and me, we got it all caught up this week."

"Good, then you'll need to wear blue jeans and sneakers tomorrow. You're going with me to make deliveries."

Lanie thought back to the conversation she'd overheard last week when Reece had told his mother his plans to take her to the farms with him. She wondered if that had anything to do with Dot's insistence on helping get the work completely caught up. If she and Reece had been a more likely pair, she might suspect Dot of matchmaking.

Then she remembered that it was Dot who had suggested Reece ask her to the banquet. Perhaps the dear old lady was sneakier than those innocent blue eyes might lead one to believe. But the very thought of Lanie and Reece becoming romantically involved was ridiculous. Even Reece thought so. Hadn't he adamantly rejected his mother's suggestion?

The warmth that crept up her neck and flooded her cheeks had nothing to do with the dog-day heat of early August. Lanie suddenly realized Reece was waiting for a response.

"Uh, okay, I'll wear jeans tomorrow."

"Great."

Lanie reached for the door handle, but he wouldn't move. He was acting like the dates who'd lingered at her door, trying to finagle a good-night kiss. Please, no. Not now, not here. Not so close to bedtime when she'd surely replay it in her dreams all night. "Is . . . is there something else?"

"Yeah, um . . ."

He hesitated, then leaned a little closer. Lanie braced herself, helplessly anticipating a kiss that would knock her stockings off. Like their first kiss almost a week ago . . . the kiss that had haunted her, invading her thoughts until it seemed that every time she was around Reece she acted like a graceless imbecile.

". . . about that dinner you're inviting my mom and Walter to . . ." Reece rubbed his knuckles across the little indentation in his chin. "How's Sunday at two o'clock?"

Lanie sighed.

Fortunately Reece mistook it for reluctance rather than remorse over a missed opportunity. "Look, you don't have to—"

"No, I'd . . . love to have your mother and Walter over on Sunday. And you, too, of course."

Her thoughts flitted through the preparations she'd have to make. She must be insane to expect people to eat her cooking. Maybe Etta would cater it. No, that wouldn't do— Dot said she overseasoned everything. Then inspiration struck.

"Do you suppose they'd like spaghetti and salad?" That should be fairly simple—even for a kitchen klutz such as herself.

"Sure, sounds great."

Maybe not great. She'd settle for edible.

As soon as Lanie and Winnie set foot in the store the next morning, her knee-high horse took off on her daily cat chase.

"Heads up, everybody!" Lanie called out.

The cat seemed to love this morning ritual. Lanie could anticipate what would happen next. After circling a display row twice—maybe three times if he was extra frisky—the cat would leap to the top of a pile of grain sacks. Then he would arch his back and hiss at the horse.

Both animals were true to form this morning. Unbothered by the cat's theatrics, Winnie nudged his side with her nose. She kept pushing until the cat hung sideways from his perch with his claws firmly imbedded in the thick paper bag.

Lanie laughed at the unlikely friends and went looking for Reece.

She found him out back with Howard, loading bales of straw and sacks of oats into the back of Reece's pickup. From up close, the battered vehicle looked more faded red than pink. The tailgate was missing, and an array of dents and rust spots decorated the sides of the ancient machine.

One look at Howard showed he had no business lifting the heavy sacks. The older man pulled a red-checkered handkerchief from his overalls and mopped the sweat off his equally red face.

"Howard, Violet's looking for you," Lanie lied.

"All right, I'll be there in a minute." He bent to lift another sack.

"She said she needs you *now*." Lanie crossed her fingers behind her back.

Howard shuffled back into the shop, muttering something about "dadgum women," and Lanie picked up the sack he'd dropped. It was about as heavy as Winnie but more cumbersome since it had no belly for her to slip her arms under.

Reece scowled for a moment. "Maybe I'd better go see what Violet wants."

"No, don't!" Lanie heaved the sack into the truck and turned toward Reece. "I, uh, was hoping that by the time he found out Violet didn't ask for him, we would've finished loading the truck."

He frowned at her for a long moment. She wasn't sure whether it was from annoyance or the sun. *Great. Now he's adding "liar" to the list of descriptions he has for me.* Reece lifted another sack and easily tossed it into the truck.

"Thanks. He wouldn't listen to me."

They finished loading the truck in silence. When they were done, Lanie's jeans—the ones with the cute little design on the hip pocket—were covered with dust and straw. Her red canvas ducks were no better. Lanie adjusted the scarf that held her hair off her neck.

Reece tossed her the keys. "You drive, I'll navigate. May as well learn your way around the county."

Her prayers had been answered. When he'd first mentioned the idea of Lanie coming along with him on deliveries, she'd feared that a scenic drive in the countryside would stir up the romantic thoughts she'd fought to suppress. With her mind on driving and her eyes on the road, she'd have little opportunity for such daydreams.

Cursing her peripheral vision for allowing her tantalizing glimpses of his muscular legs, she shoved the key into the ignition. "Where's the *perndle* indicator?"

"The what?"

"Prndl. You know...that gizmo over the steering wheel." He stared at her in incomprehension, so she spelled it out for him. *"P. R. N. D. L. Perndle."*

"Oh, that." He rested his arm along the back of the bench seat, and Lanie was acutely aware of the closeness of his fingers. "It doesn't have one. It's a manual transmission."

"Good grief. I guess that explains the three pedals on the floor."

Reece slumped back in the seat and stared straight up. He rubbed the back of one clenched fist across his forehead. "Don't tell me. You don't know how to drive a straight shift."

"Well, you don't have to get so melodramatic about it. I hear it's not that difficult to learn."

"Yeah, and I'm the lucky guy who gets to teach you." Reece didn't even attempt to keep the sarcasm out of his voice.

"Ten bucks says I can learn to drive this piece of junk."

"Without stripping the gears or wrecking it?"

"Sure. I may be klutzy, but I'm not dangerous."

Reece sat up and turned to face her. "If you're so sure of yourself, let's raise the ante. If you can't drive this truck by Monday, then you'll owe me one huge favor, payable on demand."

Lanie's mouth opened. What was he suggesting? "You don't mean—"

"Nothing illegal or immoral." He held his thumb and forefinger close together. "Just one itty-bitty huge favor. Deal?" He stuck his hand out for her shake on it.

Lanie didn't know whether to be relieved or disappointed. Not about the illegal part. But common sense told her it was safest to rule out the immoral stuff, as well. She ignored his gesture and situated her purse on the seat between them. A safety barrier.

"And if I win?"

"Same deal. One itty-bitty favor. But nothing illegal." His grin was one of such pure mischief that Lanie had to wonder which was the real Reece—the stern, solemn-faced employer, or the devilish little boy she'd seen surface in him several times. She admired the reliability of the employer, but she sure did enjoy the little boy in him.

"One *huge* favor, and you can rule out immorality." His crestfallen look didn't faze her. Her house needed a fresh coat of paint, and here was just the man for the job.

Reece pretended to spit in his palm before they shook hands. He seemed smugly certain she would lose this bet. But Lanie was determined to win. This was the perfect opportunity to show him that she didn't turn *everything* she touched into a mess.

Howard came out to give Reece the clipboard with the delivery slips attached. As Lanie, following Reece's directions, slipped the truck into gear, he hollered for Howard to stand clear. That was all it took to rattle her nerves. The truck lurched, shuddered once, and then stalled out.

Once she got the vehicle on the road at cruising speed, driving it wasn't so difficult. She had to keep reminding herself not to ride the clutch. Actually, Reece did plenty of reminding, too. He had scooted to the middle of the seat, presumably to help, but Lanie suspected he wanted to be close enough to take over the controls at a second's notice. She tried to ignore the virile male hovering at her elbow.

"You're acting like this is a brand-new Lamborghini. Relax. I won't put any more dents in your precious truck."

Reece leaned back against the seat and made an impressive attempt to look relaxed. In an almost-casual tone, he said, "My father gave me this truck when I got my driver's license." He chuckled softly. "I used to call it the Masardi-mobile."

Lanie slowed down as they rounded the bend at Folsbee's Market. No wonder he was so uptight. As beat-up as it was, this truck must be a reminder of happier days, before his father had gotten sick.

"Was it pink then?"

He made something of a snorting laugh. "Yeah. No amount of polishing would make it red again. It's a good thing I was on the football team, or I'd have never lived it down."

Lanie was uncomfortably aware of Reece watching her downshift as they approached the intersection where she was to take a left. She was a little long coming off the clutch, but otherwise she was catching on quickly. He finished giving her directions to the Wertzle farm, and she pulled in with a minimum of grinding.

A woman with long, brown hair came out of the white farmhouse. She was holding a baby and had a small boy by the hand.

"Reece," the woman called, "I thought it was you. Karl's in the barn with Number Twelve. He's been out there since sunup, but she hasn't dropped it yet."

Reece got out of the truck and crossed the yard to the porch. It was too hot to wait in the truck, so Lanie hopped out and joined them. Reece tweaked the baby's bare toe, then lifted the boy over his head before introducing the two women. "Lou and I have known each other since grade school," he said, apparently trying to ignore the kid that was jumping up and down and jerking his arm.

"Uncle Weece, let's go see the calf get borned. Mama said maybe it's twins!"

Reece turned the question to Lanie. "Wanna go see a calf 'get borned'?"

"In real life? I've never seen anything give birth before!"

"Y'all go have fun. I've got work to do," Lou said, waving them on. "But come inside for a cola after you're done."

Reece shook himself free of the boy long enough to tease his friend. "Add some banana-nut bread, and we might consider it."

Lou smiled and retreated into the house.

The kid yanked his arm again and half dragged him toward the barn. "Come on, Weece, before she pops it out."

Lanie gasped. Certainly he wasn't going to let the child witness such an event! Reece stopped on the path to the barn and turned around to wait for her.

"Don't you think he should wait outside?" she asked. "A three-year-old is too young to be watching Mother Nature in action."

"I'm four and a half," the kid insisted. "And her name is Number Twelve, not Mother Nature."

"It's okay," Reece said, squeezing the boy's shoulder. "Weasel here has seen it a dozen times already."

"Millions of times," Weasel corrected. The little tyke arrogantly thrust his chest forward. "I've been helping my daddy pop 'em out for *years*."

Lanie didn't like it—not one bit. But she wasn't the child's mother. She had been sheltered from the earthier aspects of life until she'd reached her teen years, when her father could no longer put off telling her about the birds and bees. Although she knew there was nothing *wrong* with his witnessing the birth, she still felt the urge to cover the child's eyes.

"Well, I guess farm kids grow up faster," Lanie muttered in resignation. She followed them into the barn and hesitated at the box stall until her eyes adjusted to the dim light. She opened the door and stepped inside. When her eyes focused on what was happening, she wished Reece had decided to stop at this farm last. Preferably *after* the calf was born.

The cow's head lay at Lanie's feet. Its eyes showed bewilderment, but no fear. A short, stocky man was tending to the animal. Lanie considered getting sick, but opted for keeping busy as a means of distraction. She knelt behind the cow's black-and-white head and soothingly stroked its knobby forehead. Then she called Weasel away from the animal's legs lest it kick out in pain. The boy came and knelt beside her.

"You sure you never saw nothing get borned before?" he asked Lanie.

She shook her head, trying not to notice what was going on at the other end.

The boy was clearly astonished. "Are you kidding?"

A masculine snicker drew her attention to Reece, who was kneeling beside her at the animal's midsection, his hands splayed out on its heaving flank. Reece grinned, his eyes never leaving Karl. "Hey, Weasel, she can't drive a truck, either."

"Hooo, man! Where'd you find her?"

This time, both Reece and Karl laughed.

What was with these men? Did they think no other lifestyle existed outside their own? She figured they'd certainly feel out of place on *her* turf.

"Well, answer me this, how many of you boys have ever slid down a laundry chute? Can you ride a wheelie and do doughnuts on a skateboard? Hmmm?"

"We don't have laundry chutes," said Weasel. "And there's nowhere to ride a skateboard."

"Just as I thought," said Lanie. "I'll bet none of you have ever ridden a bus downtown, either."

"*Au contraire*," Reece said, lifting one finger. "When I was Weasel's age, my parents drove me to Southside Plaza. Then we rode the bus downtown to the Miller & Rhoads department store to see Santa Claus."

Lanie was amazed. That must have taken well over an hour and a half, one way. For her, the trip to see Santa had been a five-minute wait at the bus stop and a ten-minute ride downtown. No wonder Dot saved all her errands for an all-day trip to town. And no wonder so many home gardeners were willing to pay the slightly higher prices at Masardi's to save themselves a trip to the bigger stores in town.

"Damn." Karl wiped his arm and hands on a towel and sat back on his heels. "She's going to lose it if we don't do something quick."

Reece rubbed the cow's belly. "Breech?"

"No. It's in position, but I could only feel one hoof. The other must be down near its chest."

Number Twelve groaned as if in response to the hopeless sound in Karl's voice. Lanie stroked the animal's sweaty neck. Why did she have to come with Reece, today of all days? If anything happened to the cow or her calf, Lanie knew she wouldn't be able to hold back the tears. She couldn't help it. She was that type of person. She cried at sad movies, too.

But this was different. This was life and death. This was reality. In reality, Number Twelve could be steaks on the Wertzles' table if she didn't make it through this. Veal, if the baby didn't make it. Lanie looked down at the bovine's face, its gentle brown eyes full of trust. They couldn't just sit here and wait for them to die. They had to do something.

"Let's call the vet," said Lanie. "You know, the one who specializes in . . . cattle." She cut herself short.

Weasel was trying, without success, to tempt Number Twelve with a handful of hay.

Reece stood and started unbuttoning his shirt. "He'd never make it in time. Karl, let me try."

They switched places. Lanie considered it a wise move. From up close, she could see just how short Karl's arms were. She thought Reece tactful not to have mentioned that fact.

Once again, Lanie was awestruck at the sight of Reece's bare chest. The Shirtless Wonder. Dark golden curls feathered his pectorals, circling the nipples and trailing to the navel and below. Beads of perspiration gathered and trickled down the middle of his abdomen. Lanie felt the strangest urge to wipe it off. Her grandmother had once said, "Horses sweat, men perspire, and ladies glow." Lanie decided she must be phosphorescent by now, and she knew it came from more than the August heat and humidity.

"When I say 'pull', you get out of there. If you don't, the contractions could break your arm." When Reece nodded his assent, Karl positioned his hands on Twelve's abdomen. "You hold her by the halter," he told Lanie, "and whatever happens, don't let her get up."

Reece noticed her grim-lipped determination. Satisfied that she wouldn't panic under fire, he did as Karl directed. His fingers touched a nose, then a tiny hoof. He pushed farther. Feeling the chest, he searched for the other leg. The pressure tightened on his arm, and Karl told him to "pull."

On the next try, Reece wasted no time. He searched desperately for the retracted leg. The heavy barnyard smell filled his nostrils. Sweat trickled down his nose, and he fought the urge to sneeze.

Once again, Karl gave the order to pull out. "The contractions are coming harder and faster," he told Reece. "If you can't get it this time, we'll have to sacrifice the calf. Number Twelve is young and healthy. She can have more."

Reece thought he heard a gasp, but in the next instant he was back inside, groping for the calf. "Come on, Masardi," he muttered to himself. "Three strikes and you're out." His hand closed around something. He prayed it was the leg he'd been searching for and tugged. At the back of his mind, he imagined he heard a lullaby.

"Pull," said Karl.

"I'm pulling, I'm pulling," Reece huffed.

"No, dammit, I mean pull *out!*"

The pressure on his arm was excruciating, but after what seemed like an eternity, he felt something give. In the next instant, the calf glided smoothly toward the light of day. With a soft plop, it landed in the straw.

"You can let her go now," Karl told Lanie. It was then that Reece realized she had been singing a lullaby to Number Twelve.

The heifer lumbered to her feet and sniffed her new baby. She went about the business of cleaning the bull calf.

"Wow! He's a big one," Weasel squealed.

In a flash, the youngster darted past Number Twelve to take a closer look at the newborn. But the new mother didn't see it that way. The boy's jerky movements must have seemed threatening to the heifer. She lowered her head toward the little intruder and pawed the straw in warning. In his eagerness to pet the new calf, Weasel appeared not to notice the danger.

Reece moved toward the boy, hoping to get between him and the cow. There wasn't time; she was lunging for him!

Reece grabbed for the halter, knowing he was too late. She was almost upon him when she stopped short, as if startled by something. From the corner of his eye, Reece saw Lanie yank the cow's tail again with all her might.

When Twelve turned her attention to Lanie, Reece grabbed the boy and tossed him to Karl like a sack of grain. Karl set Weasel on top of the stall partition and quickly hoisted himself over. Reece heard the stall door slam shut. Number Twelve had barely avoided a collision with the door after Lanie had escaped.

Now the cow turned a wild eye on Reece.

Chapter Five

Reece slowly retreated until he touched the back wall. Twelve charged. Reece faked right, then cut to the left and took the wooden partition headfirst. He felt his body scrape from chest to knees over the rough wood, and landed, with a thud, on his side.

"Oh my God! Reece, are you all right?"

He eased over onto his back, gulping air into his lungs. A brown-haired angel hovered over him. He peered at her through pain-squinted eyes. Surely he'd died and gone to heaven. But did angels wear designer jeans and form-fitting shirts?

Lanie knelt beside him, fumbling with the scarf that held her hair in a now-bedraggled ponytail. She freed the red cloth and gently—ever so gently—blotted the perspiration from his face. She tried to recall what her first-aid book said to do in a case like this. Mouth-to-mouth? No, he was breathing, however belabored. With each ragged breath he took, she ached for him. Had she the ability, she would gladly suffer his pain to spare him.

"Reece, can you hear me?"

Weasel wormed his way between them. He leaned close and peered at Reece. "Is he dead?" the boy asked matter-of-factly.

Karl easily lifted the youngster into his arms. "No, he's not dead. Just got the wind knocked out of him."

"Can I call 911? Can I, Dad? I know how to do it."

"No, but you can go ask your mom to get out the cream we put on your boo-boos." Karl set his son down and affectionately swatted his small behind as Weasel took off for the house.

Lanie unfolded the cloth and dabbed at the mixture of sweat and blood that stained Reece's chest.

"Aaagh!" Reece forced himself to a sitting position and stopped Lanie's ministration with a hand on her wrist. "Don't you know... better than to rub... salt into an open wound?" he panted.

Lanie sat back on her heels, startled yet pleased that he was conscious and able to sit up. But he didn't have to be such a grouch. "I was only trying to help," she said, unable to keep the peevishness out of her voice.

He released his iron-hard grip on her wrist and leaned back, his elbows resting in the clean straw. "Please don't kill me... with your kindness."

At that, Karl burst out laughing. "Don't worry about him, missy," he said, resting a reassuring hand on her shoulder. "He'll be just fine. C'mon, let's get the ol' cattle dodger up."

With much groaning and straining, Reece allowed them to help him to his feet. They guided him to the barn door, but as soon as he set foot on the red clay path leading toward the house, he waved them off. "Don't want the kid to think I'm hurt."

Lanie hid a smile as she thought of Weasel's disappointment over not being allowed to call the rescue squad.

When they reached the porch, Reece grasped the rail and eased himself up one step. With the other hand, he reached for Lanie's shoulder. Despite the heat, his touch sent shivers down her spine. Instinctively she looped her arm around his waist to steady him. She tried to ignore her feeling of contentment at the intimate contact, and mentally chastised herself for finding pleasure in the situation.

True, she had vowed to keep a respectable distance, physically and emotionally, from the man. But this was the charitable thing to do, she rationalized. However, it was something other than charity that made her aware of the firm abdominal muscles expanding and contracting under her fingertips as Reece labored up the steps.

Karl opened the screen door, and Reece stepped away from Lanie. There was little time to mourn the void it left, for Lou hustled Reece to a chair in the kitchen and thrust a warm, wet washcloth into Lanie's hand. "Clean him up while I get the salve," said Lou. "And Karl, would you rock the baby to sleep?"

"Can't. Gotta check on the calf." He turned to Lanie and Reece on his way out and lifted his thumb in salute. "You guys are all right." Then he was gone. Like a shadow, Weasel was close behind his father.

Lou came back with the cream and handed it to Lanie. "That was man-talk for 'we appreciate what you did to protect Weasel.' I don't know why men can't just say what they feel." She went to the oven and took something out, talking all the while. "Weasel told me what happened. You two make quite a team." When she came back, she placed two plates of what looked like some kind of cake on the table near them. The aroma was heavenly. "Better let this cool a minute. Do you suppose you cracked any ribs?"

Reece straightened in his chair and gently eased the washcloth from Lanie's grasp. "No, I don't think so. It doesn't hurt bad enough to be a crack. Probably just bruised."

"You ought to know. I'll never forget that game in our senior year when half the Fairton football team piled on top of you and broke two of your ribs."

As Lanie recalled how Reece had dodged the maddened cow, she gave silent thanks for his football experience.

"What I don't understand," said Lanie, "is why Number Twelve charged us. Before that, she had been so gentle, even with all the things Karl and Reece did to her."

Lou took the washcloth from Reece and flung it toward the sink. "This was Twelve's first calf. Maternal instinct must've kicked in kind of strong. It happens sometimes." She lifted the baby from the playpen and took her from the room.

Lou's singing drifted to them from the baby's room. Reece handed Lanie the tube of antibiotic cream. A barely suppressed grin deepened the creases of his cheeks. "It hurts when I move."

Lanie wondered if he was faking. She dismissed the notion with the reasoning that he was probably in too much pain to enjoy her doctoring. Even so, she felt uneasy about it. Slathering a washcloth over that stupendous chest had been one thing. But without the barrier of the fabric—a defensive shield—between her fingers and his skin, she feared she might want to touch more than his chest. She remembered his kiss, the feel of his lips on hers, his fingers gently resting on the small of her back. Even without a mirror, she knew her cheeks were pinkening.

She gritted her teeth and squirted a glob of cream onto her fingertips. As she smoothed the salve over the reddened areas of his chest, he never flinched.

"Don't forget here," he said, pointing to an angry red nipple. When Lanie hesitated, he feigned innocence. "It hurts," he insisted. "You don't want it to get infected, do you?"

She sighed. He knew all the right strings to pull, and he wasn't above using that knowledge. But to what end?

She honestly didn't know. Reece had no interest in her. She'd known that since the day he'd adamantly rejected his mother's suggestion to ask Lanie to the banquet. True, he'd joked around with her and made teasing innuendos as he had the day he'd removed her splinters. But as much as she tried to downplay the attraction that sparked between them, she couldn't explain away his reaction to their kiss. He'd been as deeply affected as she was. Of that, she was certain.

She recalled Howard's words the day he'd accidentally intruded on their conversation. *It's about time.* Had Reece been without a woman's company for so long he would have reacted that way with any female?

She pushed aside the thought and touched the cooling salve to his skin. Massaging the spot he indicated, she worked the cream past the thick sprinkling of golden hairs and into the scrapes. Against her will, she noticed his physical reaction to her touch. Though she was tending only to the injured nipple, both had risen to hard, round pebbles in response to her gentle caress.

Reece reached out, his fingers closing around Lanie's hand and placed her palm above the unhurt left nipple. She could have danced a Mexican hat dance to the fast-paced beat of his heart.

Lanie frowned. "I had no idea your run-in with Number Twelve frightened you so. Your pulse is racing like a runaway train."

Reece closed his eyes and drew in a slow, harsh breath. When he opened them again, he turned his chocolate-brown gaze on Lanie. He seemed only fractionally more composed as he removed her hand from his heart. He cupped her small hand in both of his.

"Frightened? No." He shook his head. "Terrified is more like it."

A sad smile touched his lips.

"It's like your whole life flashes before your eyes," he said, "and you think, 'I've lived thirty-one years and it has to happen like *this?*' One wrong move and *wham,* she almost rips your heart out. Kinda makes you wonder if God's just playing a big joke."

Lanie wasn't certain who *she* was, but she doubted Reece was referring to the cow. Their eyes connected. Windows to the soul, her grandmother had called them. Lanie couldn't name what she saw in those windows, but for some reason the glimpse unsettled her. An uncomfortable feeling passed through her, and she slowly withdrew her hand from his.

"I made that banana-nut bread especially for you, and you haven't even tasted it," Lou said as she entered the room and crossed to the refrigerator. Retrieving the butter and two colas, she then plucked a knife from the drying rack and set the lot on the table between them. "You expect me to treat you like company or something?"

Lanie and Karl unloaded the Wertzles' order from the truck. The rest of the deliveries were made quickly with Lanie and the farmers doing the lifting. A disgruntled Reece waited in the truck cab at each stop, barking instructions to

Lanie. She shrugged off his gruffness, chalking it up to his aching ribs and feeling of helplessness.

Lanie steered the truck to the back of the shop and braked to a slightly jerky stop. She smiled in satisfaction at the progress she'd made with just a half-day's practice at driving it. She might win the bet after all.

Walking ahead of Reece, she reached out to open the door for him. But before her fingers touched the knob, the heavy metal door swung open. Violet emerged and tossed the gray cat like tepid dishwater onto the grassy lawn.

"Go catch a mouse," she admonished. "Make yourself useful." Violet briskly brushed her hands together as if ridding herself of an unsavory pest. Tucking a stray hair under her trademark triangle scarf, she turned to Reece. "Don't ask," she said. "Just follow me."

Lanie and Reece exchanged glances and followed her into the store. Lanie got the sinking feeling that, whatever had happened, Winnie was behind it.

Sure enough, Winnie stood tied to Lanie's desk. The long rope allowed the animal to roam outside the office, but when Violet picked up a broom, the little horse quickly retreated.

"She's kinda skittish 'cause I swatted her once on the backside," Violet explained as she turned her attention to the grain sacks cluttering the floor.

Lanie groaned.

Reece muttered something unrepeatable.

Since Lanie had started bringing Winnie to the store, the staff had made certain there was always a pile of bags for the animals to curl up on. Usually it was grass seed or fertilizer where they'd found a place to sleep. Today it had been horse feed.

Grain spilled from a dozen or more bags onto the speckled tile floor.

Lanie put a hand to her forehead as she surveyed the mess. She knew Reece wouldn't be out of line if he fired her for this.

Her glance flew to the obvious culprit of this crime. Winnie's ears perked forward, but the black mischief-maker dared not step a foot out of the office, not with Violet wielding the broom so close by.

Reece picked up a new shovel from the rack and started scooping the loose feed into a wheelbarrow. Lanie could see him grimace with pain each time he lifted the heavy weight.

She put a hand on his arm to stop him.

"Please, Reece, you shouldn't exert yourself. Let me do that. It's the least I can do."

He hesitated long enough to throw her an angry look, and went back to shoveling. "Why don't you just take your horse and go home," he said.

She was right. He was firing her. But she couldn't let this happen. This job was too important to her. It would be impossible to earn enough at a temporary agency to pay the mortgage on her house. And that was *if* she could get a job at all after losing three jobs in a row.

But there was more at stake than money. This was the first time she'd worked for a small, family-owned company. Here, in the course of only two weeks, Lanie felt like an integral part of the operation. She'd already implemented a few procedural changes that had streamlined inventory control. And she was thinking ahead to ways in which the accounts could be computerized. Reece couldn't let her go now. He needed her, even if he didn't know it yet.

But even more, Lanie knew, she needed this job. What other company would let her bring her horse to work with her? Still, after today, even if she managed to talk Reece into changing his mind about firing her, she might no longer be able to enjoy that fringe benefit.

And more than missing the fringe benefits and job satisfaction, Lanie knew that leaving Reece—not seeing him every day, not looking for him, however surreptitiously, when she arrived each morning—would hurt the most. She'd no longer wake up each morning full of anticipation and eager to start the day.

How had it come to this point in just two short weeks? It was wrong for her to feel this way about Reece, she knew. They were too different, too incompatible. Even their sun signs said so.

Maybe it was best that it end this way. In the long run, she'd be freed of a lot of agony.

Lanie stepped over the scattered grain. In the office, she picked up her coffee mug and unfastened the lead from Winnie's halter. "Come on, nuisance. Let's go home and replan our future."

With a heavy heart, she left the tiny office that had become her domain. She had even heard Reece tell Howard one day to leave some order forms in "Lanie's office."

She stiffened her back and slowly walked past where Violet and Reece were still cleaning up. Winnie gave wide berth to Violet and her broom.

"Reece . . ."

He lifted another shovelful and dumped it into the wheelbarrow. Breathing hard, he set the shovel down and rested one forearm on the handle. The eyes that held hers were no longer angry, but neither were they cordial. They looked weary, and Lanie knew she was to blame.

The feeling of togetherness they'd experienced in the barn today and afterwards when she'd tended his scrapes had dissipated. Now, Lanie felt like the enemy.

". . . I'll pay for all the broken bags. My checkbook is at home . . ." She trailed off as she suddenly realized her account held nowhere near enough to cover the cost. Maybe he'd let her pay for it over a period of time. Now, however, was not the time to ask.

"Wait a minute." He dug into his pocket and extracted the truck keys. "Would you mind driving me home? I'm not exactly in shape to shift gears." He tenderly touched his side.

"Sure, I'd be glad to, but my car—"

"It'll be fine here," he said, handing her the keys. "Besides, you're going to need the weekend to practice driving the Masardi-mobile. Howard, you'll close up for me, won't you?" he called out. "Thanks. I'll see you Monday."

Howard gave him an incredulous look. "You're not working tomorrow?"

"Nah. I've got a project to take care of." He touched a hand to the small of Lanie's back and guided her outside to the truck.

When he opened the truck door, Winnie leaped in and clambered over toward the driver's side.

"The horse rides in the back," said Reece.

Lanie got in and poked the keys into the ignition. "Don't be ridiculous. Winnie always rides up front with me. Of course, it appears that there are only two seat belts. I don't suppose you could share yours..."

Reece flung her a scowl that could have melted granite.

"I didn't think so." Lanie glanced back at the truck bed. The missing tailgate left an opening that looked as dangerous as a mountaintop precipice. She could easily picture her curious horse nosing close to the edge and then being pitched out as the truck took a curve.

"No. I can't let her ride back there," she said finally.

Reece peered at her from behind the hand he'd rested his forehead on. "Why not? Barney always rides in the back."

"Barney?"

"The cat. We found him in the barn behind the shop."

"Oh." An odd feeling of relief settled in her at the knowledge that Reece had named the cat. At least he wasn't so rigid that he'd let his pet go without the social amenity of owning a name. "Why don't *you* let *Barney* ride up front?" she countered.

"Did once. He got under the brake." Reece straightened and then leaned against the elbow support on the door. "The big dent on the right front fender is my memento of the event."

He took a deep breath and sank into the seat, closing his eyes as his head came to rest against the cracked red vinyl upholstery.

As big as he was, his posture reminded her of a little boy of long ago. A picture of her youngest brother filled her mind. Her family had driven home at dusk, after a picnic supper following an exhausting day of swimming at the lake. Donnie's eyes, puffy from sunburn and water, had slowly drooped closed. When the six-year-old's head had nodded forward against his chest, Lanie had slipped her arms around his small shoulders and cuddled him close. Though only ten at the time, she'd felt protective toward all three of her brothers.

For some unfathomable reason, she felt the urge to slip her arms around Reece's shoulders and lay his sleepy head against her breast.

Lanie sighed. Dragging her eyes away from the sleeping man-child, she cranked the engine. It took three starts to find first gear, but the rest of the drive home was uneventful.

Walter's Lincoln occupied the driveway across the road. Lanie thought she noticed a movement of Dot's curtains but ignored it as she hopped out and focused her attention on opening the truck door for a groggy Reece.

"Thanks," he said as she handed him the keys.

She stood for a moment, wondering whether to follow him in and . . . and what? Tuck him in?

What was the matter with her? Here it was, less than an hour after she'd been relieved of her job and what was she doing? Trying to play nursemaid to her ex-employer! It led Lanie to wonder which she was more deficient in—common sense or pride.

Probably both.

Reece had unlocked his front door but didn't go in. His eyes caught hers and held them. For a long moment they regarded each other, until Reece broke the silence.

"I assume you did okay driving us home since it looks like we arrived here in one piece. Maybe you'll win that bet after all." A weak smile touched his mouth but didn't quite reach his eyes. "I'll feel more like coaching you tomorrow, but right now I'm bushed. Guess I overdid it with the shovel."

How could he do this—act like nothing had happened? He had *fired* her, for crying out loud.

"Look, Reece, why don't we just forget this silly bet. I'll ask Dot to give me a ride to my car. There's no reason for you to—"

"We made a bet," he said firmly. "If you back out now, you forfeit and I win. Are you prepared to pay off?"

The terms of the bet had been that the loser deliver one huge favor. If she won, she could forget the paint job and demand a second chance at her job. And since the bet only ran until Monday, she might not even miss a day of work.

"We made a deal," she said. "If I win, I'll expect you to pay off as promised."

"Masardis never welsh."

* * *

It started out as restlessness. When it progressed to hiccuping and pacing, Lanie grew worried. By midnight, Winnie was thrashing and pawing at the living-room floor.

Something was desperately wrong with her, but Lanie didn't know what. What was the name of that veterinarian? She flipped rapidly through the Bliss phone directory, but the words all seemed to run together.

She picked up the phone and dialed Information. "Please, I need the number for the veterinarian in Bliss County," she told the operator.

"The name?"

"I don't know! Can't you just tell me if there's a vet with a Bliss exchange?"

"One moment, please."

"Please hurry!"

Winnie groaned and lay on her side, her fuzzy black body lathered with sweat.

"Still checking," said the operator.

"Forget it." Lanie hung up the phone and dialed the first three digits common to all Bliss phone listings. Maybe Reece would know what to do. Hadn't his father run a farm when Reece was a kid? And he had seemed very competent when helping deliver the calf.

Were the last four numbers 4763 or 6743?

Winnie groaned again.

Lanie slammed down the phone in frustration. "Don't worry, baby," she soothed her pet, "Mommy's going to get help."

She shot out the kitchen door and took the rail fence like a track star. Racing up the porch steps two at a time, she simultaneously rang the bell and banged on the door.

"Reece, wake up!" She rapped her knuckles against the door until they were sore.

Reece finally appeared, hair rumpled and clad only in undershorts. Flipping the porch light on, he squinted down at her, taking in the thin cotton nightgown that barely concealed her curves. His eyebrows furrowed together in apparent confusion.

"Reece, are you awake?" She snapped her fingers in front of his face. "I need your help."

Her panicky words must have penetrated his foggy brain. He grabbed her by the upper arms, his fingers pinching into her soft flesh.

"What's the matter? Are you okay?" he demanded.

"It's Winnie. She's sick."

His grip on her arms relaxed, and Reece rubbed where he'd held her.

"Go stay with her. I'll be there as soon as I find my pants."

He was only a minute behind her, but it seemed more like hours. Lanie sat cross-legged on the floor, holding Winnie's head in her lap and trying to calm the frantic horse when Reece burst in. In her agony, the little animal moved her hooves repeatedly.

"It's the colic," said Reece. "Get some mineral oil. Then we'll take her outside to walk her."

"Walk her! She can hardly stand. Can't you see she's suffering."

Reece grabbed the lead from the top of the oil circulator that dominated the living room. Snapping it onto the halter, he said, "That picnic your horse had today is coming back to haunt her. I don't want to worry you, but I've seen horses die of colic. It's especially dangerous in one as young as Winnie."

He bent and lifted the horse from her lap.

"We've got to keep her moving," Reece said in a gentler tone. "If we let her lie down, her gut will twist."

Lanie grabbed the mineral oil from the pantry. She followed him out into the yard, fear seeping into every part of her body, and helped administer the dose.

Winnie was the last thing her father had given her. Lanie had bottle-fed her, gotten up every couple of hours to feed her when the animal was younger. She loved the little rascal. If anything happened to her...

Winnie's squeaky cries tore at her heart. She couldn't just sit here. She had to do something.

Reece set the horse on the ground and motioned for Lanie to grab the halter strap behind Winnie's right ear. Winnie immediately collapsed.

Lanie's first impulse was to let her lie there. Anything to alleviate the animal's pain. But she remembered Reece's dire prediction. She steeled herself to what must be done.

She pulled her pet's head up. In her firmest, scolding voice, she commanded the horse to "Get up!" Each time Winnie balked, Lanie scolded again and firmly jerked the halter. Lanie winced even as she did so. After this was all over, she would try to make up for the sharp words.

At first Reece appeared surprised by Lanie's tone. It soon became evident that Winnie obeyed better and seemed less frantic under her authoritative tone. He smiled his approval.

Around and around the old shade tree they went. Lanie guessed they must have circled it twenty times by now. She looked at Reece, patiently taking step after methodical step. His broad shoulders drooped from exhaustion, but he never once complained. They walked side by side, the horse between them. Reece lightly touched a hand to his chest, and Lanie remembered.

"You shouldn't be doing this," she said. "You're bruised. Here, let me." She reached for the rope, but he held tight.

"I'm fine," he said and kept walking. After a couple more trips around the tree, he said, "Winnie was a gift from someone special."

It wasn't a question. He was confirming what she'd already told him.

"Yes." Winnie slowed, and Lanie tugged until she was walking again. "I miss him a lot."

Reece looked at her for a long moment, his expression unreadable in the dim light filtering from the kitchen. He reached up and rubbed a hand along the back of his neck.

"This...someone special. Do you mind my asking where he is?"

What he really wanted to ask was why anyone would go off and leave a girl like Lanie. Even if the guy intended to come back for her, he was taking a chance by turning her loose without a wedding ring. What man wouldn't be attracted by the way she tried to hide her weaknesses behind a curtain of super-efficiency? A man could easily lose himself in those big hazel eyes. A man could fall for the quiet sensitivity underneath that bumbling exterior.

It was a good thing he knew better than to let down his guard around her. He knew the danger of getting involved with someone like Lanie, and he would sidestep the possibility whenever it arose. Strangely, it bothered him to think that she was involved—or had been involved—with someone else. Her someone special obviously cared about her a great deal. And she about him.

Buck up, Masardi, he told himself. *She's taken. That should make it easier to stick to your resolve.*

"I believe my father's in heaven," she said. "He—"

Winnie suddenly anchored her hooves in the dirt and answered nature's call.

Lanie stopped walking. "Is...is it over? Is she going to be all right?"

Reece smiled. "The crisis is over. She may have a belly-ache for a while, but she'll be fine."

Lanie made a small noise. It was something between a hysterical giggle and a cry of relief. Then her hands flew to her face, and she was sobbing. In the next moment, against his better judgment, he went to her and took her in his arms.

"Shhh. There's no need for tears now."

He led her back inside to the sofa and sat down beside her, stroking the dark, shiny hair that fell softly to her shoulders. It smelled like honeysuckle. He tucked her head against his chest and dropped his hand to the tight spot between her shoulder blades. A tension knot. He'd had enough of them to know.

Slowly, gently, he applied pressure to the muscle. He rubbed his fingers in small circles on her back. Like a cat, she arched against him, the thin nightgown doing little to disguise the delicate curves and intricacies of her body. His own body reacted in a way he knew could only cause trouble if he followed through.

Reece took momentary pleasure in the knowledge that it had been her father who had given her the horse. Winnie hadn't been a lover's gift after all.

His resolve shot to smithereens, he lowered his head and kissed the living daylights out of her.

Chapter Six

Lanie's lips tingled and, oddly, so did other parts of her body. She'd been kissed before, but never like this. There was nothing gentlemanly or civilized about it. The kiss said, *Me man, you woman.* And she had never in her life been more glad to have been born female.

Now that the danger was over and Winnie was going to be fine, Lanie wanted to lose herself in Reece's kisses.

His lips circled hers in a nibbling motion while his fingers did wonderful things to the middle of her back. Ever so slowly, he claimed her lips again. This time the kiss was almost tentative. His mouth, warm and firm, forayed over her lips, kneading and suckling like a babe at his mother's breast.

Forgetting all caution, forgetting her pledge to remain uninvolved, forgetting everything but the headiness of his kiss, Lanie opened to the moist tongue roaming over her lips.

By now her heart was beating erratically. Raising a hand to Reece's bare chest to brace herself against the unfamiliar emotion sweeping over her, Lanie felt the rapid *thump-thump, thump-thump* of his heart against her fingertips. Her fingers trailing across the tangled gold curls, she brushed the abrasion he'd received in his skirmish with the cow.

With a sharp intake of breath, Reece lifted his lips from hers. For a moment, he gazed down at her, his eyes plundering her very soul. In that instant, she knew he must have seen the secret she'd tried to hide from him...the secret she'd tried to hide from herself.

With a slam, Lanie shut the windows to her soul, but it was too late. He had already seen through them. She averted her eyes, trying without success to avoid the truth.

Her hair fell in a curtain across her face. Lanie gladly took refuge behind it. Anything to keep from looking into those knowing brown eyes.

So now he knew that she cared for him. It had been a mistake to think she could work with Reece and live next door to him without falling victim to the intangible something that sparked between them.

A naive fool. That's what she was. Lanie mentally called herself a few other choice names as well.

Reece's fingers brushed her cheek as he swept aside the veil of hair and tucked it behind her ear.

Instinctively Lanie pulled away from him. "Winnie...I'd better go let her in." She made a move to get up, but Reece's grip tightened on her waist.

"Let her sleep outside tonight."

Reece snuggled down into the plump cushions and lay his head against the armrest. He drew Lanie down beside him until her head rested on his shoulder and her body nestled in the cramped space between him and the back of the overstuffed couch.

"Your ribs," she protested.

"Are fine." He draped a heavy arm over her. "Let's just rest a minute, and then we'll check on Winnie."

Cuddled comfortably between his long, hard form and the mushy pillows, her body told her not to argue. But, crazily, her thoughts veered back to her school days and the wide circle of friends whose company she had enjoyed.

"I like playing with you," her best friend, Tracey, had told her one day in second grade. "You always think of fun things to do." Shortly after that declaration, Tracey had broken her ankle and Lanie had sprained her wrist while both tried to climb a tree with roller skates on. Lanie's idea, of course. The children at school had laughed when they learned what happened. "That's what happens when you play with Zany Lanie," her friends had said. And each had a tale, and maybe a scar, to prove it.

This time there would be no scars. This time she knew the perils that came with playing this dangerous game. And this time she would say no to temptation, sparing them both the pain that was sure to follow.

She looked up into the face of temptation. His eyes were closed, and his breath puffed softly against her cheek. What she wouldn't give to be able to lie here in his arms forever. But if they were both to get out in one piece, she'd better nip this in the bud.

"Reece, I don't think—"

"Don't think," he murmured and pulled her closer.

That was the problem. Usually she didn't think. And now that she tried to correct the error of her ways, reliable, dependable, think-it-through Reece had sunk to her level of irrationality. She had obviously corrupted him.

Mere seconds later, Lanie fell asleep in the comfort of his arms. Each of the dreams that followed featured Reece in the starring role. In one, he dived headfirst over a cliff. When Lanie tried to stop him, he grabbed her, taking her with him to the inevitable crash landing.

In the next dream, she saw him carrying a tiny infant. The baby's fair skin contrasted with Reece's deep bronze coloring. The baby cried and squirmed against his chest, but Reece never grew impatient. He rubbed its tiny toes and continued pacing the floor, his deep, soothing voice lulling Lanie as well as the young child. It felt so right, with just the three of them. Reece was such a good father. The deep voice persisted, only this time he was talking to her instead of the baby.

"Lanie."

"I'll take the baby now," she murmured. "You get some sleep."

A deep chuckle penetrated the edges of her consciousness. Lanie woke to see Reece kneeling on the floor beside her, his brown eyes full of amusement.

"Oh, hell—pardon me." Instantly awake, she mentally kicked herself for giving in and agreeing to "just rest a minute." Sunlight streamed in through the window sheers. "We should never have done this."

"Done what? Did I miss something?" He looked disappointed.

"We *slept* together!"

Reece punched one hand into the other. "Damn, I *did* sleep through it."

Lanie swung a fringed pillow at him. She sat up, her feet touching the cool, hardwood floor. "Keep both feet on the floor at all times," Grandma Weatherford had reminded her before each of her few dates. Knowing Lanie's proclivity for impulsiveness, Grandma had no doubt worried that she would let reason fly to the winds in that area of her life as well. But what Grandma must have overlooked was the fact that Lanie always did the right thing.

Last night, however, she hadn't.

Lanie glowered at Reece, knowing she shouldn't hold him responsible for her own temporary lapse in judgment. She probably shouldn't hold him responsible, either, for the way he was looking at her right now. Surely the mint-green nightgown she wore left little to his imagination as his dark eyes swept over her. Self-consciously, she crossed her arms over her chest.

"I swear," he said, palms held skyward. "I didn't *knowingly* ravish your body last night. If I did, I'm sorry." The little white lines at the corners of his eyes disappeared as his eyes twinkled. "Mostly sorry that I don't remember it," he amended.

"Reece! I'm serious. What happened last night...well, let's just say it can't happen again."

She toyed with the bit of lace on the hem of her gown. Reece got up off his knees and sat beside her on the couch.

"We're too different, Reece. Your life is orderly, from *A* to *B* and all the way down the line to *Z*. My life is alphabet soup. When I wake up each morning, I never know what I'll find in my spoon." With a wry laugh, she added, "And this morning I found *you.*"

"Look," he said, laying a hand over her fidgeting fingers. "Don't you think you're making a big deal out of nothing? I agree with you that it's ridiculous to even think about us...starting something...you know, together. Sharing a couple of little kisses—"

Terrific kisses, she thought. And what did he mean, making a big deal out of nothing? Was that all it meant to him?

"—doesn't make us lovers. We both had an eventful day. We just needed a little physical reassurance."

She could have sworn he enjoyed their kisses as much as she had. That there was more involved than just hormones calling to each other.

"But there's no reason we can't be friends," he continued.

Just like there's no reason I can't be president of the United States, she thought.

"So why don't we both shower and get dressed—in our respective houses, of course—then meet in my driveway in, say, twenty minutes? You're already late for your second driving lesson." He squeezed her knee and stood up. Lanie followed him to the door.

"Reece, under the circumstances—"

"There are no circumstances, remember?" Reece opened the front door. Across the road, the curtains moved in Dot's living-room window. Funny, but Lanie didn't detect a breeze in the open doorway.

"Make it thirty minutes, and you're on."

Reece stopped and turned around to face Lanie. "By the way, you'd better not waste any time feeding Winnie. I caught her nosing around the trash can when I went out to check on her this morning."

He was, indeed, a friend. Regardless of what else might be going on beneath the surface, Reece had definitely been a friend last night. Who else but a friend would get up in the middle of the night and stay with her until her horse was feeling better? He could just as easily have told her what to do or given her the name of a local animal doctor.

"Um, I seem to have forgotten my manners." She stepped out onto the small porch. Picking a chip of white paint off the banister, she said, "You were very kind to come over and help me with Winnie last night. Thanks...*Friend.*"

"That makes us even. I forgot to thank you for risking getting the stuffing kicked out of you to save little Weasel. Thank *you*, Friend." He leaned over and kissed her lightly on the cheek, his day-old whiskers rasping across her skin. "See, nothing to it."

He turned and jogged across the yard. Lanie watched him side-hop the fence before she remembered she was standing in her nightgown on the front porch.

When Reece learned Lanie planned to gather signatures on her petition while on their outing, he sulked. Lanie was glad Winnie had been content to stay in the backyard and play with Barney. At least she wouldn't have to argue with Reece about letting the horse ride up front.

"Do all males of the human species go to school to learn how to do that?" she asked.

"Do what?"

"Sulk. My brothers had it down to an art, my father sulked around my grandmother, and now you're doing it. It must be a conspiracy."

Reece had the grace to look ashamed. In turn, Lanie tried to be inconspicuous about her signature gathering. After she had been driving for about an hour, she said she needed to stop at the grocery store for spaghetti ingredients.

Just as she'd hoped, the store was packed with Saturday-morning shoppers. She left Reece waiting in the truck, and she returned a short while later with tomatoes, peppers, onion and a page full of signatures. She even recruited a couple of volunteers to help with the *Stop the Highway* campaign.

Lanie drove where Reece directed, being careful to shift gears at precisely the right instant. She still had a little trouble on corners, but Reece patiently talked her through them. He even pointed out a number of historical homes and told the background of each, but Lanie was concentrating so hard on driving that she wasn't able to enjoy the little tour.

As they passed the forestry tower, Reece told her of the time he took a dare and climbed to the top, walking backward up two hundred steps. Armed with spray paint and an instant camera, he initialed and dated the hatch door while his high-school buddies watched from the ground. Then, as proof, he took a picture of the underside of the firewatcher's small room. He descended the steps, the paint can in one coat pocket and the camera in the other, to find his friends gone and the local sheriff waiting for him.

"What happened then?" Lanie asked.

"He went easy on me. Instead of pressing charges, he made me paint the underside of the tower house. Then, as a community service, I had to paint an elderly lady's house. Sheriff Thompson even made me buy the brushes and stuff with my own money." Reece pointed for her to take the next left, which brought them back to Sanderson Road. "From then on, I've hated painting. I'd hire somebody before I ever pick up a brush again."

Lanie smiled as she recalled the original "huge favor" she'd planned on winning. But more than having her house painted, she wanted her job back. She smoothly turned onto Judestown Road and headed for home. She felt confident she would win the bet after all.

"I would never have guessed you'd do such a thing," she said. "Weren't your parents mad?"

"Nah. When the sheriff took me home, all they said was, 'What'd he do this time?' "

Lanie took her eyes from the road long enough to see the look of pure mischief on his face. He had apparently enjoyed his escapades.

The man was a contradiction.

How could this serious, solid pillar of the community have been a teenage hoodlum? What had caused him to change from a prank-pulling hell-raiser to a striving, hard-working, no-nonsense adult? Whatever the reason, this glimpse into his past helped explain the brief uncharacteristic behavior he had displayed recently.

"The only time my parents really got mad," he continued, "was when I spent the night in jail."

Lanie couldn't believe her ears. The childish prank had been hard to swallow. But going to jail—that was something altogether different. "What did you do?" she prodded.

"Took the flag from in front of Etta's restaurant and replaced it with a bed sheet." He chuckled softly. "I had drawn a skull and crossbones on it."

Lanie laughed. She pulled into his driveway and barely missed hitting the mailbox.

"It was a pretty good drawing, too, if I say so myself," he said, bravely ignoring her near miss.

She parked the truck and looked at him, still finding it hard to believe he had been telling these tales about himself. "What happened?" she asked. "What made you change?"

His brown eyes darkened briefly, and his eyebrows returned to their almost perpetual scowl. His answer was curt.

"I grew up."

During church services, Lanie wondered if she shouldn't have stayed home to prepare for her guests. No, she assured herself, two hours should be plenty of time in which to make spaghetti and a salad and tidy up the place.

In her desire to serve a perfect meal to her guests, she worried about all the things that could go wrong. Lanie recalled the tuna casserole she'd made for herself last week. It wasn't until after she'd pulled the dish out of the oven that she had remembered the tuna. The unopened can had sat on the countertop, right where she'd left it.

Today, she promised herself, everything would be perfect for Dot and Walter. And, of course, Reece.

In the parking lot after services, Lanie managed to get a few more signatures for her petition before accepting a ride home from Dot.

She should have listened to her hunch and stayed home to make the spaghetti. As she threw together the ingredients, she realized she'd forgotten to buy a jar of sauce at the store yesterday.

Well, today she could let nothing distract her from her task. There was no time to go to the store. Lanie usually made do by dressing up prepared foods with seasonings and fresh vegetables. Today, she would have to improvise even further. She peeled the tomatoes and nuked them in the microwave. While they were going through the meltdown phase, Lanie tore up lettuce and chopped vegetables for a salad.

But when she combined the ground beef with the tomatoes and seasonings, it still didn't look like sauce.

She stuck it back in the microwave and zapped the mixture for another few minutes. The schoolhouse clock on the kitchen wall seemed to tick faster. Frantically, Lanie searched the pantry and refrigerator for something to thicken the concoction.

Ketchup!

As luck would have it, Reece chose that moment to appear at her back door. Feeling more self-conscious than usual, Lanie fluffed her hair and let him in.

Instead of his usual shorts and casual shirt, he wore a white, burgundy-striped shirt with a coordinating tie and dark blue slacks. He carried cheesecake artfully decorated

with graham crumbs and cherry topping. Seeing his creation and having him find her in the middle of her latest
blunder, Lanie felt one-upped.

"My contribution," he said. With the casualness of
someone who visited often, Reece walked to the refrigerator and set the cheesecake on the bottom shelf. "Can I give
you a hand?"

"Yeah, cover your eyes."

Lanie squirted ketchup into the tomato-and-beef mixture. Then, uncapping the bottle, she poured the entire
contents into it and stirred. Better. Much better.

"Do you always make spaghetti sauce this way?"

"Only when I have company coming in twenty minutes
and I don't have a jar of the real stuff. It's still too red, don't
you think?" Another search through the refrigerator turned
up an assortment of spices and flavorings. "This should
balance it out."

"You don't expect us to eat that, do you?"

"I *told* you to cover your eyes." She continued doctoring the sauce.

"How about some barbecue sauce to go with that?"

"Don't be gross. Why don't you make some lemonade?"

A moment later, Lanie turned around to see a nicely
shaped backside protruding from her refrigerator. It was all
she could do to keep from pinching him.

"What are you looking for?" she asked.

"Lemons. Where do you hide them?"

"You Aries always take everything so literally." She
reached into the pantry and handed him a package of lemonade mix. "You can jazz it up with a spritz of bottled
lemon juice. Fools 'em every time."

By the time Dot and Walter arrived, she had camouflaged the sauce with mushrooms, garlic and onions. It didn't taste half bad.

Dot *oohed* and *aahed* over the "heavenly smells" while Lanie got out the dishes.

"You'll have to serve yourselves from the stove," she told her guests, "because my table isn't big enough to hold everything."

It could barely accommodate the four of them. After everyone else was seated, Lanie squeezed into the empty chair between Walter and Reece. Her knee banged into Reece's leg.

"Excuse me," she said.

He'd been giving Walter the once-over, and he tossed her a questioning look. "What?"

"I kneed you," she explained.

Dot choked on her lemonade. Walter solicitously patted her back while Reece groped for words.

"What I meant was—"

"My goodness," Dot said to Walter after she'd caught her breath, "didn't I tell you they'd been making googly eyes at each other?"

"Can't say as I blame them," Walter responded. "Lanie's a lovely girl, and Reece must have inherited all your good traits." He patted Dot's hand.

Lanie admired him for his diplomacy.

"My knee..." She persisted in trying to clear up the confusion. "What I was trying to say—"

"And she's a good cook, too. This spaghetti is delicious." Walter nodded his agreement. Lanie gave up trying to explain. "Elaine, honey, you must tell me what you use to give it this unusual flavor."

Reece's fork stopped midway between his plate and his mouth. It was a good thing he hadn't taken the bite yet.

From the look he threw Lanie, he might have sprayed the mouthful across the table.

Lanie kneed him again, this time on purpose. Silently she threatened him against letting her blunder out of the bag. It was bad enough that he was wise to her cooking shenanigans. If Dot knew, she might laugh about it to the whole county. And Lanie certainly needed no help spreading her Zany Lanie reputation.

"Well, uh, I didn't really measure anything."

"I never do," said Dot. "Sometimes my best recipes happen purely by accident."

Reece coughed and covered a less-than-discreet smile with his napkin. Lanie cast him a warning look, but when their eyes met, her frown melted. For a fleeting moment, they knew the pleasure of a shared secret. The knowledge isolated them from the older couple and strengthened the delicate bond that had grown between them.

"Lanie mentioned earlier that her spaghetti sauce is a secret family recipe," Reece told his mother.

"Oh, then I won't pry any further," Dot promised.

Lanie smiled her thanks to Reece. He smiled back and gave her a conspiratorial half wink.

"See, they're doing it again, Walter!"

Lanie rose abruptly from the table. "Would anyone like lemonade?" She poured herself another glass.

"Dot, you're embarrassing the kids," Walter chided.

"Oh, they're not embarrassed. If they can smooch on the front porch for all the neighbors to see, then my little comments shouldn't bother them at all. Isn't that right, Maurice?"

Incredibly, under all that tan, Reece managed to blush. Somehow, Lanie didn't figure him for the blushing type.

Reece loosened his tie. "Mom, there's quite a distance—not to mention a few trees—between Lanie's front porch and your house. Maybe you didn't see what you thought you did."

"I didn't say it was Lanie's front porch," she accused.

"Dot, you told me yourself that your eyesight isn't what it used to be," Walter interjected.

Dot daintily wiped her lips and set the napkin on the table. "A person can see more than constellations with that telescope I borrowed from you, Walter."

"Mom! You spied on us!"

"Yeah," said Lanie, looking pointedly at Reece. "How dare she."

Reece clammed up. Although Lanie didn't like being spied upon any more than he, she thoroughly enjoyed this unexpected turnabout. What was good for the goose was good for the mother.

"Not that I'm criticizing, mind you, but you really ought to be more careful," said Dot. "The neighbors talk, you know."

"And since you live across the road, that makes you a neighbor, doesn't it?" Walter smiled good-naturedly and patted her hand again. "I thought the reason for this visit was so they could grill *us,* not the other way around."

They took their desserts into the living room. Walter regaled them with tales of his days as a military investigator. He was probably in his sixties, but looked only fifty. Lanie decided that Walter and Dot made a perfect couple. Every so often, they'd exchange knowing looks or an affectionate touch. Without a doubt, Lanie knew they were in love, and she felt happy for them.

Even Reece seemed to approve. At first he'd bristled when Walter had wrapped his arm familiarly around Dot's waist, but soon Reece warmed to the older man's congenial personality.

Surreptitiously, Dot continued to interrogate Lanie and Reece about how they'd spent their weekend. Then she turned her attention to Lanie.

"What are your plans for the future, Elaine? Do you want a large family?" Dot looked hopeful.

Dot had been asking Reece similar questions as well. Lanie was beginning to suspect, not for the first time, that Reece's mother was trying her hand at matchmaking. Obviously the older woman was trying to make something out of that "just friends" kiss on the porch.

"Mom, I don't think Lanie wants to discuss—"

"Nonsense. She doesn't mind. So, how many children *do* you want?" she persisted.

Lanie sighed. The truthful answer was not what Dot wanted to hear. Nor was it something that Lanie wanted to address. The sad fact was that Lanie was not cut out to be a mother. She couldn't even keep her mind on target long enough to make a simple spaghetti dinner. How could she expect to feed a baby nutritious meals?

"I guess I'm a nineties kind of woman," she told Dot. "Children don't seem to be in my future."

Reece seemed intent on picking lint particles from his slacks.

Momentarily stunned, Dot sat silent. She quickly resumed stride. "You'll change your mind. Once that biological clock starts ticking, babies will be all you can think about. Mark my words. Why, if Maurice hadn't been such a big galoot, he would've had six or seven younger brothers and sisters."

Reece quit picking lint and jerked his attention to his talkative mother. "Mom, don't tell that story again. We just ate."

"Oh, Maurice, you've been such an old fuddy-duddy ever since your father got sick. When are you going to learn to

loosen up?'' Then, despite her son's scowl, she proceeded
to tell the details of his birth.

The next morning, Lanie and Winnie waited by the old
pink truck for a ride to her car. Reece came out of the house
and tossed her the keys.

"Wait a minute. I've already won the bet," she declared.

"The deal was that you'd learn to drive by Monday
morning. How do I know you haven't forgotten how to shift
gears since Saturday?''

"All right. I'll show you." She took the keys and climbed
into the old truck. There was no way she'd let him weasel
out of this bet—or giving her back her job. Winnie made
herself at home between them. Reece scowled, but he didn't
object. Good, at least they wouldn't start off with an argument.

Lanie backed the truck out of the driveway, concentrating all the while on when to apply the clutch and shift to first
gear. That was when the left front fender rubbed the mailbox.

Darn! Lanie glanced at Reece, hoping against hope that
he hadn't noticed the faint scraping sound.

He had.

His dismay was immediately apparent. Lanie felt her
stomach twist, both at damaging his treasured truck and at
losing the bet. Swiftly the look on Reece's face changed to
one of triumph. He jumped out of the truck and went to
inspect the damage.

Lanie's heart sank to her feet. She didn't want to look for
another job or even work as a temporary secretary. She liked
her job at Masardi's and wanted to stay there. From the
gleeful expression Reece now wore, he planned on her pay-
ing up big-time.

He'd been annoyed with her on Friday after Winnie had ransacked the grain. This definitely was far worse. She had scratched the truck his father had given him. No doubt his "big favor" would involve asking her to leave and never come back.

She got out to see for herself how bad it was. A long white line now merged with the numerous dents and rust spots. That wasn't so bad. To see it, a person would have to get as close as Reece, who now knelt beside the front tire to trace a finger along the telltale scratch. The revelation gave her confidence.

"That sound we heard—I think it was the tires crunching on gravel," Lanie declared.

Reece smiled back at her and slowly shook his head.

Maybe if she was insistent enough, he'd believe it. "What makes you think *I* put that scratch there? It could have been there all along." Lanie folded her arms across her chest and arrogantly looked down at him.

Reece stood up, clearly quite smug with himself. "The scratch isn't rusted like the others."

Lanie lifted her chin a little higher. "So?"

At that, Reece stepped beside her and slipped his arm around the small of her back. With a little pressure on her hip, just enough to send tiny tremors through her veins, Reece guided her to the mailbox. He bent and pointed to a speck of pink paint clinging to the corner of the box.

No, she couldn't let him win this bet. Not with the stakes she had riding on it.

"It doesn't matter," she argued. "The original terms were that I'd learn to drive this tub of rust by Monday—that's today—'without stripping the gears or wrecking it.' Your words, not mine. I haven't stripped the gears, have I?" At his cynical smirk, she plowed forward. "And, technically, I haven't wrecked it since this isn't something you'd report to your insurance company. Therefore,'' Lanie continued before she ran out of steam, "I demand that you honor your end of the bargain. You owe me one huge favor."

There. Let him dispute that.

Suddenly aware that his hand lingered on the curve of her back, Reece stepped away. "I guess if you want to get technical about it, we both won this bet. What do you say we both pay off?"

He was curious as to her demands. Since he was the one who had set the terms, he'd just have to take his lumps if she insisted on doubling her salary or asking for something equally outrageous. He steeled himself, preparing for the worst.

"Deal," she said. He took her proffered hand in his and marveled at its softness. "I want my job."

What? Had he missed something? "The job is yours," he said.

Relief washed over her features, and Reece only now noticed how tense she'd been.

"Thank you. You've lived up to your end of the bargain, and I'll live up to mine. Ask away."

Chapter Seven

Reece hesitated. This had been too easy. Why had she asked for something that was already hers?

His mind raced back over the events of the past few days. Had he somehow given the impression he didn't want her working for him? Admittedly she was slightly loony, but her work was exceptional, just as she'd promised that first day. In fact, in just two weeks she'd proven herself to be even more organized and more productive than his own mother. And that was no simple feat.

"No funny business, Masardi. You promised nothing immoral or illegal."

He let his eyes sweep over her, taking in the way her turquoise suspendered slacks cinched tightly at the waist, the straps molding over the soft curves of her bright jungle-print shirt. She was not too lush, not too skinny. Any man would be proud to have her on his arm.

He'd probably live to regret this.

"Okay," he said. "You're going to the Bliss Banquet with me next month."

Lanie studied him for a long moment before answering. True, she owed him whatever favor he asked. But she knew he didn't want this particular "favor." Hadn't they both agreed it was ridiculous to consider a relationship outside of friendship?

"Look," she said, "I know your mother put you up to this, so why don't you ask for a favor you really want?"

Distractedly he rumpled his hair. Lanie noticed how the dark hairs underneath contrasted sharply with the sun-bleached strands on top. Her gaze took in the perfectly arched eyebrows that were every bit as dark as the hair untouched by the sun. She imagined herself trailing sensitive fingertips over those brows that resembled a hawk's wings, and raining light kisses on the darkly fringed lashes rimming those delicious chocolate eyes. Ordinarily she didn't care much for sweets, but chocolate had always been a weakness of hers.

When she realized where her thoughts were taking her, she quickly reined them in. Reminding herself that they'd wisely agreed to be just friends, she waited for him to rescind his request and think of another.

"I need a date," he finally admitted, "and I didn't know who else to ask."

If she'd been insulted before, she now felt mortally wounded. To think that he'd asked her to accompany him because his mother had suggested it had been bad enough. But to be told that he had only considered doing so after exhausting all other possibilities was humiliating, "just friends" or not.

"Oh, right," she said, making no effort to suppress the sarcasm in her voice. "Go ahead and flatter me."

"Lanie, that's not what I meant."

He reached for her, but she sidestepped him and flounced into the truck. "The back end of this truck is hanging out onto the road. We'd better go now." She slid over to the passenger side and positioned Winnie between them. "You drive—I'm too rattled."

Let him wonder whether she was blaming her nerves on his comment or on having scratched his truck.

Reece slipped into the driver's seat and restarted the engine. "I didn't mean that the way it sounded. But you did agree to the terms of the bet, and I expect you to pay up."

"What about all that talk of our being just friends?"

"Nothing has changed. For the past two years, I took my mother to the banquet. This year I'm taking a friend. Okay?"

She wasn't wild about being lumped into a category with his mother. But if they were to continue to work together and remain good neighbors, it was best they learn to get along as casual friends.

"Okay," she said. "Maybe I'll even meet some nice local fellas while I'm there."

Reece ground his teeth and spun the tires in the loose gravel.

Lanie's petition and letter-writing campaign proved successful. At the next meeting of the Board of Supervisors, the *Stop the Highway* group won a small victory when the Board agreed to hold the issue as a special referendum after the upcoming Bliss Festival Week, which ended on Labor Day weekend.

During the month of August, Dot seldom showed up for work at the shop. "You're doing just fine," she'd told Lanie one day. "Why should I come get in your way when I'd have a much better time touring Charlottesville or Williamsburg with Walter?"

Lanie was happy Dot had found companionship in someone whose personality complemented hers as well a Walter's did. Maybe someday Lanie would find happiness with a man suited to her own quirky traits. Lanie sighed when she considered the possibilities. There was enough self-induced confusion in her life. Why should she want a man with the same faults to add to that confusion?

She and Reece spoke to each other in a most professional manner, their responses almost stilted in their efforts to keep a safe but cordial distance.

Still, though her behavior was proper, her thoughts were not. Effortlessly her mind roamed back to the weekend Winnie had gotten sick. More than once since then, she'd awakened to the memory of Reece holding her to him, his heavy lids closing in weary slumber. She tried to steer her wayward imagination far from the thought of how it would feel to wake up in his arms every morning. And she tried to filter from her mind the more scandalous image of Reece's body bearing down on hers as he made slow, excruciatingly tender love to her.

Whenever her longing became too painful, she reminded herself of their differences and of the sad but agonizing fact that he didn't want her. He'd as much as said so.

Sure, they'd kissed a couple of times. Thirty years ago, that might have meant something. But in today's era of self-gratification, kisses meant nothing—no matter how good they'd been at the time. As Reece had said, it had been nothing more than a physical need for reassurance after an event-filled day. Lanie just wished her body would stop wanting his reassurance.

"Aha! I caught you at last, you little cheese snatcher."

Lanie peered down into the plastic wastebasket at the rodent circling the bottom. She debated whether to retrieve the wooden ruler that had served as a makeshift gangplank, but decided against putting her hand too close to the mouse. However, if she left the ruler in there, the mouse might be able to climb up and jump out.

Barbecue tongs! She turned her back long enough to rummage through a kitchen drawer for the tool. When she turned her attention back to the mouse, she found Winnie with her nose in the wastebasket, her ears pricked forward in curiosity.

"Get out of there, you goofball." Lanie pushed her away. "Do you want to get bitten?"

Lanie grabbed the ruler with the tongs, but not before the vermin made one last bid for freedom. It skittered up the ruler and leaped almost to the rim of the basket.

Lanie squealed, flinging the tongs and ruler across the kitchen. She stepped back, her heart pounding as if she'd been chased by a wild rhinoceros.

A knock sounded at the back door. Lanie whirled, her half-slip billowing above her knees.

Oh, no. Reece was here already, and she hadn't even finished dressing. At least she'd put on the top half of her dress before the mouse had fallen into her trap. She let Reece in and walked over to pick up the tongs and ruler.

"You don't need to cook," he joked. "They'll feed you at the banquet."

Lanie tossed the tongs into the sink and threw the peanut-butter smeared ruler in the trash. Then she noticed Reece—*really* noticed him. He wore a soft gray suit that seemed to magnify the broadness of his shoulders. The neat white shirt was tucked into the waistband of his slacks. Why were they even bothering to go to the banquet? He looked good enough to eat.

"I, uh, didn't expect Mickey over there to take the bait until I was gone. Give me ten minutes, and I'll be ready."

"Make it five," he called after her. "I don't want to be late."

Lanie went to her room and glided the slim tiger-striped skirt up over her hips. She fastened the matching black and silver belt around her waist and was digging in her jewelry box for a silver necklace when she heard Reece swear.

"What's a mouse doing in your trash can?"

Without even bothering to unfasten the strand, she slipped the pendant over her head. When she went back to the kitchen, she found Reece standing over the wastebasket, staring down at the jailed mouse.

"How'd you get him in there?" he demanded.

Lanie was enormously pleased with herself for having invented a humane trap, so she didn't mind sharing her discovery with him.

"I knew the mouse had been on the counter, so I baited a ruler with peanut butter and balanced it here on the edge. When he walked out to get the peanut butter, he and ruler fell into the wastebasket."

She gave Reece a smug smile. But he only stared back at her, as if she were some strange new species that warranted further study.

"Haven't you ever heard of conventional methods? Folsbee's Market sells mousetraps and poison. Why didn't you try something like that?"

He seemed angry, and Lanie had no idea why. Jeez. He was acting like she had committed a crime by being unorthodox. Well, by now he should know better than to expect her to do things in a "normal" way.

She grabbed her clutch purse and tucked it under her arm. Her chin rose along with her annoyance. "What difference does it make to you how I catch a mouse? I got the job done, didn't I?" She pressed her lips together. "I didn't want Winnie to get poisoned or her nose pinched in a trap.

Besides, it's kinder to the mouse, too." She picked up the pink wastebasket and walked to the back door.

"Where are you going with it?" he asked.

"We're going to set him free in the woods."

He pushed back his cuff. "Look, it's getting late. Can't you do that in the morning?"

"He might starve!"

"Well, put some cheese in there, for crying out loud."

"Reece, the poor little thing is terrified. I can't just leave him in here to die of shock. And Winnie keeps trying to play with him. What if he has rabies and bites her?"

Reece pulled at the knot in his tie. "All right," he said, reaching for the wastebasket. "I'll run it out back and turn it loose."

"Thanks for the offer," said Lanie, "but he's already figured out how to get in my house. We'd better take him somewhere else so I don't have to go through this all over again."

Reece groaned and ran a hand through his neatly combed hair. He took the basket from her and closed the back door, making sure to lock it. "I'm parked out front," he explained when she raised questioning eyes to his.

"Then why didn't you come in the front door?"

"Only company comes in the front way."

He held the door for her, and she stepped out to find an elegant white Jaguar parked in her driveway.

"Oh, Reece, it's beautiful. When did you get it?"

Or, more precisely, *why* did he get it? She found it hard to believe that this exotic sports car belonged to the same man who had clung to the dilapidated pickup truck for so many years. When Howard had approached him about buying a new vehicle for the shop, Reece had refused, saying there was no need since the truck was still running. He hadn't mentioned wanting a new car, and Lanie couldn't envision him buying something like this on impulse.

Reece anchored the wastebasket between their seats and held the door for Lanie. The rich black leather smelled fresh and new as she settled back into the seat. He walked around and slid into the driver's seat.

"It's not mine," he said as the engine growled to life. "Mom bought it yesterday—don't ask me why." He shook his head in incomprehension. "The truck needs some work, and since Walter's taking Mom to the banquet in his Lincoln, she lent me this."

"You sound like you don't approve."

"I just wish she'd shopped around more. I would've tried to talk her into something more sensible."

He skillfully maneuvered the car out of the driveway and headed out Judestown Road toward Sanderson Road. Then he took a side road to a secluded area and pulled in at a small wayside.

"My father and I used to hunt here. Back then, nobody lived for miles around." Reece took the wastebasket and was preparing to empty the mouse into the ditch.

As gracefully as she could manage in the tight skirt, Lanie got out of the car and picked her way across the scattered leaves, twigs and vines growing alongside the road. "What if he runs out into the road and gets smashed by a car?"

Reece stopped what he was doing to stare at her, one hand on his hip and the other trying to rub the consternation from his brow. It was so quiet out here Lanie could hear the mouse's feet skittering across the bottom of the plastic container. "All right, I'll take it farther into the woods." Then he muttered something about being late for the banquet.

"I'll do it." Lanie took the little trash can from him and marched off toward the thick of the woods. Her heels sank into the loose dirt, and bits of brush snatched at her nylons. Something crashed through the woods behind her, and she turned to see Reece running to catch up with her.

"You didn't have to come. I can take care of it myself," she said.

The deer path they followed was too narrow for them to walk abreast, so Reece followed close behind. They'd walked a short distance when Reece finally spoke—to Lanie. He'd been muttering under his breath all along. Lanie had tried to ignore the deep rumble of his voice, chalking his mumbling up as another skill all men were born with. Like sulking. But she found she liked the depth of it, the way it vibrated and wound its way into the corners of her mind.

"I doubt he'll find his way back to the road from here without a compass and knapsack. Or did you plan to provide them for him?"

Lanie halted and uttered an oath of her own. These shoes were meant for sidewalks or carpets or polished floors, not for tramping through the forest. She'd come close to falling more than once, and for what? For a little mouse, who'd probably end up as an owl's meal anyway. Even so, she was doing the right thing, and she was glad of it.

"Lighten up. I'm setting him free now." Lanie turned the wastebasket on its side and watched the gray mouse scramble into the underbrush. "Bye, Mickey," she said and gave a little wave.

A boom reverberated through the woods. If that was thunder, it had struck something close by. Reece's hand closed around her arm.

"I didn't see any lightning—"

"Shhhh."

From off in the distance they could hear a man shouting. And he didn't sound happy. Another boom rang out.

"Let's get out of here." Reece started off the way they'd come, but Lanie didn't budge. "What are you standing there for? He's got a gun!"

This time he grabbed her arm and didn't let go. Together they ran, Reece pulling and Lanie trying her hardest to keep up despite her confounded high heels. Nimbly he skirted a broad old tree, but Lanie wasn't as agile. The pointed toe of her shoe caught an upgrown root and she went sprawling. She fell against Reece's back. Instinctively her arms flew around his waist, but her momentum had pushed him forward. She slid down as he flew forward, her face grazing his rear end, his thigh, and his calf during her graceless tackle.

In a flash he was up, hauling her to her feet. Then they were off again, jumping fallen logs and pushing past blackberry briers.

"Are you sure we're going the right way?" Lanie huffed. The walk in the woods seemed to have taken half as long as their mad flight out.

Reece raised his free arm and pointed. "Just over that rise."

But as they crested the rise, there was no car to be seen on the deserted road.

"Damn, I overshot it." He slid his hand down and clasped her fingers in his. They sprinted over the rough asphalt pavement around the curve to where the white car waited for them. Behind them, the gunman's footsteps crackled over dried twigs and leaves. His language colored the air blue.

In her haste to enter the car, Lanie banged her head on the low roof. The engine started right up, and Lanie gave thanks that the recalcitrant pink truck had chosen today to go on the blink. As they sped away, Lanie turned in her seat to peer out the small back glass. A grizzled mountain of a man stood beside a No Trespassing sign, shaking the gun over his head.

Lanie faced forward and let out a shaky breath. Her body sagged against the black leather. After a minute or so, Reece slowed to a normal rate of speed. "Are you okay?"

Lanie assessed her damages. "I think so. Just kind of messy."

Reece was no better. Dust clung to his elbows and knees, as well as the entire front of his dark gray suit. His shoes were scuffed, and a bit of vine dangled from his hair.

"My trash can! We left it in the woods."

Reece took his eyes from the road and let his gaze wander over her dishevelment. He shook his head. "Let him have it."

"I don't think pink is his color."

A muscle twitched in his jaw. Reece rubbed the back of his neck. "Lanie, is it just when I'm around, or does stuff like this happen to you all the time?"

"Stuff like what?"

His knuckles whitened as he clasped the steering wheel. "Stuff like getting shot at. Didn't it strike you as odd that a man with a gun chased us out of the woods?"

"Yeah. I guess I should have noticed that No Trespassing sign before we went on his property."

He groaned. "That's not what I mean." He glanced at her again. Except for some general mussiness, she seemed quite composed now. Was her life usually so bizarre that getting shot at seemed like an everyday occurrence? "Doesn't it bother you when things like this happen?"

"A little," she said. "But I can replace the wastebasket for under five dollars."

Reece thought, not for the first time, that it had been a mistake to ask Lanie to come with him tonight. What had he been thinking when he'd called in his bet? The original

plan had been to ask her to find someplace else for her little
horse to stay during the workday. But after Winnie had
gotten sick and he'd seen the fear in Lanie's hazel eyes, he
didn't have the heart to ask her to make that sacrifice. Winnie and Barney still made their morning runs through the
store. And surprisingly, Reece found that he was becoming
accustomed to their peculiar ritual.

But Lanie's peculiarities were another matter. Why, just
last week she'd suggested they sell grain in the old-time
flowered canvas sacks. She'd explained that the fabric would
appeal to newer residents who'd been lured to the county by
its rustic charm. Sure, her idea to expand the pet supplies
and sell horse books and figurines had proven successful.
But he'd have to give the feed sack notion some more
thought.

He stole another glance at the woman seated beside him.
Involuntarily his hand reached out to touch a silken strand
of dark brown hair.

She didn't pull away. In her green-and-tan eyes he saw a
hint of humor—the kind people share after they've weath-
ered an ordeal together. They were comrades.

Reece plucked a fragment of dried leaf from her hair.
"You're a mess," he said, and grimaced when he heard the
tone of condemnation in his voice.

The humor left her eyes, and Reece was sorry to see it go.

Lanie fixed a sugary smile on him. "Nice to meet you,
Pot. You can call me Kettle."

Reece pulled into the dirt parking lot at the Memorial
Building and took one of the few remaining spaces. "Point
taken." As he walked around to open the door for Lanie, he
dusted himself off. Taking her arm in his, he led her to the
massive stone steps at the front of the old building.

"Wait a minute." Lanie burrowed into her clutch and withdrew a clean, but wrinkled, tissue. "Here," she said holding it up to his face, "spit."

"Huh?" Reece took a step back, scowling at the tissue as if it were already contaminated.

"You have a dirt smudge on your cheek. Just moisten this, and I'll wipe it off for you."

He hadn't been spit-washed since he was six years old, and he didn't want to start now. He took the tissue from her and rubbed the left side of his face.

"Now you're smearing it." Lanie reached up and guided his hand to the right spot. She stood so close he could smell the faint honeysuckle scent of her shampoo. He breathed deeply, savoring her sweetness, wanting to pull her to him and make those large eyes close in anticipation of his kiss.

Reece shook the thought from his head. Lanie was a nice girl and a terrific office manager. But she was also trouble—with a capital *T*.

The last three years he'd been so busy taking care of the business he'd had no time for a social life. So perhaps it was natural for him to react this way to an attractive female, no matter how mismatched they were.

Well, he would rectify that situation. It was about time he started on his five-year plan. All he had to do was meet the perfect woman—a conventional hometown girl whose worst personality quirk consisted of leaving panty hose drying on the shower rod—fall in love, marry her and produce two-point-three well-behaved children. Tonight, by appearing in public with a woman other than his mother, he'd be letting Bliss's eligible bachelorettes know that Reece Masardi was now available.

Still, when he remembered what Lanie had said about meeting some of the local men tonight, he clenched his teeth and stuffed the tissue in his pocket.

"Come on," he growled. "Maybe we can make it in time for dessert."

Lanie followed him into the crowded civic-center-turned-banquet-hall. So now he was back to being moody. She'd known he wasn't exactly happy about the mouse incident, and even less so about the irate property owner. But he'd mellowed for a moment. That moment when he'd looked at her, his expression soft and gentle, she'd thought they would make peace.

Maybe it was best, she decided as they took their places near Dot and Walter. Each time Reece had become Mr. Nice Guy, she'd weakened and rashly allowed herself to indulge in the pleasure of his closeness, his touch, his kiss. With any luck, he'd remain cool and aloof, and she wouldn't need to wrestle with her impetuous nature.

"It's about time," Dot said as Lanie slid into the hard metal folding chair beside her. "Where have y'all been, in the hayloft?" She reached across Lanie and removed the vine from her son's hair. "Looks like you've been making more than googly eyes. I hope you used protection."

Heads turned at the loudly spoken words, and several folks smiled behind their hands.

"Mother!" Reece glared at Dot. It was a look that would have sent a lesser person cowering. "The only 'protection' we needed was bulletproof vests. Lanie and I are late because we were chased by a man with a gun."

Lanie heard a collective intake of breaths. Reece had spoken loud enough for all those around them to hear his explanation. Lanie wasn't sure whether he did it more to protect her virtue or to deny any romantic involvement with her.

"Maybe you should report it to the sheriff," someone suggested.

"Where did it happen?" Walter asked.

A woman from the local church group that was providing the meal placed a plate in front of Lanie. Reece waited for her to serve him before answering.

"Down Thirteen Curves Road, about three miles off Sanderson Road. You know, the old Clemson place."

"Serves you right," Dot insisted. "You ought to know better than to go necking on someone else's property."

Lanie laughed out loud. "Dot, you *do* have the wildest imagination."

Reece, however, didn't appear amused. "I'm past the age of reporting my whereabouts to you," he said through gritted teeth. "But since you seem intent on ruining Lanie's reputation, I will tell you that we were freeing a mouse she'd trapped."

"Hah!" Dot downed the last of her coffee and turned to Lanie. "And you say *I* have a wild imagination."

Dessert was served before the conversation could go from bad to worse. Lanie gave thanks for small blessings. Dot had turned her attention back to Walter and was now giggling like a young girl.

Lanie toyed with the remainder of her pie. "Your mother and Walter make a cute couple."

Reece's only reply was a halfhearted grunt.

"I thought you liked Walter."

He leaned back and stretched his arm across the back of her chair. "Yeah. Walter's a good man. It's just that ever since he and Mom started seeing each other, she's been trying to get me to start dating again." His eyes caught hers and held them captive for a moment. He averted his attention to the blue flowers adorning the edge of his dessert plate. "I'm sorry she embarrassed you. Just chalk it up to wishful thinking on her part."

Wishful thinking? Lanie had no idea why Dot would wish her on Reece. Weren't mothers supposed to protect their

young? A glance at Reece's large frame and scowling coun-
tenance discounted any notion that he needed protecting. If
anything needed protecting, it was Lanie's heart.

"Oh, I wasn't embarrassed." He quirked an eyebrow at
Lanie. "Well, not much. I consider it a compliment that she
likes me well enough to try her hand at matchmaking."

He smiled at her. Lanie snapped a mental picture. Though
she knew she shouldn't, she tucked the image away in her
heart's treasure chest. *A friend,* Lanie reminded herself. *It's
okay to cherish a friend's smile.*

Mr. Tighe, the banker who sat opposite Reece, com-
mented on the recent spate of good weather, and the two
were soon discussing the farmers' economic situation. She
turned to Dot, who was listing for Walter the merits of her
new automobile.

"It's a pretty car," Lanie noted.

Dot winked and nudged Lanie with her elbow. "Actually it's a little too extravagant for my taste, but I was hoping that Maurice would learn to like it. Maybe then he'd
loosen up a little and stop acting like an old codger." Dot
beamed with self-satisfaction. "From the looks of things
when you two came in tonight, it must have worked, huh?"

Walter slipped his hand into Dot's and squeezed her fingers. "Honey, if you want to be a mother-in-law someday,
you need to practice being discreet."

Lanie distractedly folded and refolded her napkin. "I hate
to disappoint you, but Reece was telling the truth about the
mouse." Then she described catching the mouse in her
wastebasket and setting it free on posted property. By the
time she finished telling the incident, Walter was grinning
broadly and Dot was wiping tears of laughter from her eyes.

"I believe you," she said. "There's no way you could
make up a story as cornball as that and still keep a straight

face. Elaine, my dear, Maurice needs someone like you. You keep things hopping.''

Lanie sighed. Why couldn't she lead a normal, peaceful life like everyone else? She chanced a look at Reece and saw that two other businessmen had joined in the conversation. The four were carrying on a lively debate about the proposed highway's expected impact on the county. When Lanie realized she'd shredded her paper napkin, she placed the bits on the table and folded her hands in her lap.

"That's exactly why it would never work out between Reece and me," Lanie said. "Every day there's a new disaster waiting for me to walk into it. Reece, on the other hand, has complete control over everything in his life. I'll bet he even lays out his clothes each night and makes a list of things he plans to accomplish the next day."

"You're right. The boy's hopeless." Dot wiped her mouth and set the napkin on the table. "But he wasn't always that way. Why, I was just telling Walter the other day how Maurice used to tease his daddy and me. But shortly after Albert started forgetting things, Maurice stopped being playful. It was as if seeing his daddy lose control of his behavior made him that much more determined to keep strict control over his own life."

Reece's back was still turned to them. Lanie enjoyed the rise and fall of his voice as he interjected his comments into the conversation with his friends. She felt a twinge of guilt over hearing Dot's intimate revelations about him. Even so, she was glad Dot had told her.

Now she understood why Reece had reacted so vehemently to her letting Winnie in the house, and why he had criticized her unusual mousetrap. Her unorthodox ways forced him to confront his own, hidden personality—the one he had run away from.

Dot's disclosure also explained Reece's abrupt mood changes. Lanie recalled the few times he'd let her glimpse his playful, little-boy side. Then suddenly, he'd reverted to his cool, restrained persona. And, in doing so, he'd kept her a safe arm's length away.

"You're good for him, Elaine," Dot continued. "He's smiled more since you came than he has in the last three years."

Someone blew on a microphone. Lanie recognized the man at the speaker's podium as Mr. Morrison from the Board of Supervisors' meeting. Still preoccupied with her newfound knowledge about Reece, she only half listened as he introduced himself and talked about the history of Bliss County.

Lanie remembered the way Reece's eyes had glittered with excitement as he'd recounted his days of teenage mischief. Tonight, that piece of the puzzle slid snugly into place.

Obviously his father's illness had made an enormous impact on his life. Reece had chosen to reform himself and take a more responsible route in life. That explained why he disliked Lanie's dingbatty impulsiveness.

Mr. Morrison proceeded with a lengthy discourse on the accomplishments of various members of the community.

Reece had been right. And now, more than ever, Lanie concurred with him that anything more than simple friendship would be an impossibility.

Lanie almost snickered at the irony of that last thought. Mere friendship with Reece would be anything but simple.

"...and in addition to all his other accomplishments," Mr. Morrison concluded, "I understand that he recently saved the life of a young child. Let's hear it for Bliss County's Man of the Year—Reece Masardi!"

Everyone clapped as Reece wound his way to the head table. Some people cheered, and whistles could be heard from all corners of the room.

Amidst the flashing of camera lights, Mr. Morrison handed him a plaque. Reece stood patiently until the hullabaloo died down. Lanie thought he looked embarrassed by all the attention.

"I'm surprised," he said quietly. He held the award away from him and silently read the inscription. He shifted his weight and gazed out at the attentive faces in the audience. "Of all the folks in Bliss County, I can think of many who deserve this more than I do. Just like Mr. Morrison mentioned, I've given some of you farmers interest-free credit. But in just the past couple of years you've given me far more. And I thank you for that." His voice shook slightly, and Lanie felt a lump rise to her throat. Reece held the plaque in front of him for everyone to see. "I thank you for this."

Once again, the crowd burst into applause. Lanie clapped until her hands felt raw. She reached over and hugged a misty-eyed Dot.

"That's my boy," Dot said, her voice cracking with emotion.

Mr. Morrison approached the podium to signal the end of Reece's acceptance speech. But Reece stayed.

"There is one thing I'd like to clarify," Reece said, his composure now firmly back in place. "About a month ago, Karl Wertzle's little boy was almost trampled by one of their dairy cows."

He turned and fixed his attention on Lanie's corner of the room. Lanie grew warm as realization dawned on her. She wished she could slide under the table and hide. Her eyes met his, and she implored him not to do it, but to no avail.

"Lanie, would you come up here?" he said.

Her cheeks burning, she reluctantly rose and met him at the podium. To her surprise, he laid his arm familiarly around her shoulders.

"If it hadn't been for Lanie Weatherford's quick thinking and heroic actions, I wouldn't have been able to get to Weasel in time. I think Lanie's the one who deserves your applause."

Karl and Lou Wertzle led the crowd to their feet.

Lanie forced a smile, but she felt like a fraud. There had been nothing "heroic" about pulling Number Twelve's tail to distract her. The act had been pure impulse, without a single thought to its consequences. Another Zany Lanie stunt. She didn't like the idea of being applauded for acting on a character flaw.

She moved out of Reece's grasp, and he followed her back to their table. A brash man in an ill-fitting suit called out, "Hey, Reece, I hear you're in favor of this highway thing so you can go up on your prices. You stand to make a bundle, don't you?"

Unriled, Reece responded, "If the plans are approved, Bliss will see a considerable population growth. I'd like to turn that to the farmer's advantage, Ed. We'll raise prices slightly on home and lawn products so that local farmers can buy at a reduced price." He shot a broad smile at Lanie. "Miss Weatherford here will be setting up the new pricing system. So when you come in to order your seed, just talk to Lanie and she'll see that you get your discount. And don't forget to vote *yes* on the highway issue."

In a most unladylike reaction, Lanie's jaw dropped. How dare he drag her into such a scheme! Now it looked like she supported the proposed highway.

The look she shot him told exactly what she thought.

Chapter Eight

If looks could kill, Reece would have been a dead man. Of all the times in her life when she'd embarrassed herself, Lanie couldn't remember ever having been more humiliated. Nor had she ever been so cleverly manipulated.

To make matters worse, the local newspaper ran an article that stated that "the *Stop the Highway* campaign may have derailed when outspoken opponent Lanie Weatherford switched tracks in a surprise move Friday night."

Lanie leaned forward in her swivel chair and propped her elbows on the newspaper spread open on her desk. Her head in her hands, she closed her eyes and tried to think of a way to correct the error before Tuesday night when the Board of Supervisors would hold its referendum. But, unfortunately, the weekly paper wouldn't hit the stands again until the day after the referendum.

Idly she turned the page and saw her name yet again. This article was topped with a picture of Lanie as she stood beside Reece at the podium. The piece consisted mostly of Karl

Wertzle's account of Weasel's rescue. Lanie remembered telling the reporter that her part in it had been blown out of proportion. In print, the statement made her appear modest. She frowned. Lanie certainly didn't mind taking credit when it was due, but Karl's glowing portrayal of the event made her uncomfortable.

Over still another story, the headline declared *Man of Year* Chased by Gunman.

It must have been a slow week for news, Lanie thought as she finished glancing through the twelve-page paper. The other articles covered the highway debate and the events of the Bliss Festival being held this week.

As she scanned through the festival schedule of animal judging, craft exhibits, parade, carnival and dance, Lanie came up with the perfect idea for urging folks to vote against the highway. She smiled as she closed the paper.

A light knock sounded on the office door. Lanie turned to see Reece smiling at her. She didn't smile back. Since he'd made a fool of her at the awards banquet, she'd been polite and businesslike. Nothing more.

"Elgin Thurloe is here to see you," he said, laughter glittering in his warm brown eyes. He stepped aside to allow a burly mountain of a man into the small room.

Lanie sucked in her breath. Instinct told her to dive for cover, but Reece seemed unintimidated by the man's presence. She settled for pressing her fingertips indelibly into the chair's seat edge. Unconsciously she made ready for a quick escape if he should lunge at her.

"May I help you?" she asked, her voice barely above a whisper.

"I b'lieve this belongs to you." The bearded man in coveralls pushed a pink wastebasket at her.

"Wh-why, thank you." She glanced up at Reece. He was still smiling as if he found it all amusing. "I'm sorry we trespassed on your property," she said.

"'at's all right. I thought you was highway surveyors." The gunman tugged at a fringe of beard on his chin. "So when I read that story in the newspaper, I knew I had to bring you back your trash can, miss." He turned to Reece. "If I'da known you was Man of the Year, I'da shook your hand."

Lanie set the wastebasket on the floor. "Why did you think we were surveyors? The highway's not supposed to come anywhere near your property."

The big man humped his shoulders. "Beats me. Y'all looked like city people, all dressed up and everything. Guess I just got nervous. My apologies for scaring you, miss. See ya, Reece."

Lanie stared after him as he left. "That's amazing."

"That he returned your trash can?"

"No," Lanie joked. "That he reads the newspaper."

Reece chuckled. "Elgin has a college degree."

Lanie raised an eyebrow.

"Animal husbandry. Anybody with a question about breeding goes to Elgin. He knows his stuff."

"If you knew the guy, why didn't you stop him from shooting at us? We could have been killed!"

Reece crossed his arms over his chest. Lanie's gaze took in the sinewy strength of his muscular forearms. "If you expected me to stand there and argue with his gun," he said, "you've got a lot more to learn than I thought."

Silently she agreed. She did have a lot to learn. And the first was how to be in the same room with Reece without noticing the golden hue of his tan, the broad and powerful muscles that flexed with his every move, or those little crinkles at the corners of his eyes. Maybe, with enough practice, she could learn to ignore the way she felt whenever he was around.

Saturday morning dawned bright and clear, without a hint of clouds. It was a perfect day for a parade.

Using her best penmanship, Lanie printed *Stop the Highway—Vote No* on two poster boards. She colored the letters with a red broad-tipped pen so the message would be visible from a distance. Then she connected the boards by stapling lengths of ribbon between them. Stepping back to examine the results, Lanie was satisfied it would be an eye-catcher.

And just to make sure, she went to the dresser, pulled out her star-spangled shorts outfit, and put it on. The cuffed red-and-white-striped shorts were topped by a clingy blue T-shirt with various sizes of white stars sprinkled across the front and back.

Lanie tucked the sandwich board under one arm. "C'mon, Winnie, let's go for a ride."

The wait at the high school football field proved to be a long one. And hot, too. Lanie went to her car to get Winnie a drink from the insulated water jug. In a matter of minutes, Lanie was passing out cups of water to the cheerleaders and high-school marching band and urging them to get their parents to vote against the highway proposal.

At precisely eleven o'clock, the caravan of fire trucks, floats and performers lined up and headed off down Courthouse Road. Twenty minutes later, Lanie took her place behind the 4-H Club float and proceeded to walk the mile to the judges' stand in front of the courthouse.

Heads turned and children waved, but Lanie wasn't the least bit self-conscious as she tossed lollipops to spectators. She was glad of the attention since it might help rustle up some support for the highway opposition. And Winnie didn't seem to mind, either. She trotted from one side of the road to the other, as far as her lead rope would allow, accepting goodies from delighted onlookers.

Reece cut short his comment to Harley Ferguson when the people around him pushed forward to see a parade exhibit. Out of curiosity, he stepped up on the low wall that enclosed the courthouse lawn.

"Aw, isn't that cute!" a young girl exclaimed.

Reece peered over her head. It took only one look to know exactly who and what everyone was talking about.

Trotting smartly with blue-painted hooves, Winnie wore a large sandwich board proclaiming *Stop the Highway— Vote No*. Red, white, and blue ribbons festooned the little horse's mane and tail, and she pulled a toy wagon that had young spectators clamoring for a turn at a ride.

As striking as that sight was, it was Lanie who caught and held his attention. From the red, white, and blue bow perched atop a perky ponytail, to her red canvas shoes, Lanie was a walking Uncle Sam. But instead of declaring I Want *You*, the patriotic-colored banner that flew from her broomstick pole read simply, No!

Reece's eyes returned to take in the long slender legs that extended from the cuffs of her red-and-white shorts. Even though summer was now fading, her shapely calves were only barely tanned. From her fair complexion, Reece guessed that even if she were a faithful sun-worshiper, she'd get little darker than a faint creamy beige. With a strange twinge, he realized he found her legs appealing just for the fact that they were attached to her.

His attention roamed to the body-hugging shirt. The sight brought to mind a number of road signs he'd passed on the way to the parade. Soft Shoulders. Dangerous Curves. With a sense of foreboding, he recalled another sign that summed up his feelings about Lanie: No Way Out.

Sweat had gathered between her breasts and trickled down her abdomen, leaving a dark line down the front of her blue top. Reece felt a compelling urge to go to her and pull the fabric away from her hot skin. He rubbed the perspiration from his hairline. The temperature seemed to have shot up in the last thirty seconds. With a jolt, Reece knew the Labor Day weekend sun had nothing to do with his internal fire.

And if he felt this way just from looking at her, what might she be doing to all the men on the sidelines? As much as he hated that other men were looking at her with desire—just as he had been—he knew Lanie was unaware of the effect she had on them. Still, that knowledge did nothing to soothe his jealousy. It was all he could do to keep from going to her and hauling her bodily out of the parade to insist that she cover those luscious swells with a baggy, shapeless shirt.

Reece's jaw ached, and he realized he'd been clenching his teeth.

Harley poked him with an elbow. "Hey, Masardi, isn't that your office manager? I thought you'd won her over to your side." He took his sunglasses off, wiped them on his shirttail, and settled them back on his nose. "Kinda easy on the eyes, ain't she?"

Reece ignored his friend's comments. Lanie's eyes found his. For a brief instant, her expression conveyed defiance. Then, with a smug smile, she seemed to say, *"Gotcha!"*

Apparently not expecting Lanie's hesitation, Winnie plowed into the back of her legs. Lanie lurched forward a half step before regaining her footing. Reece sighed as he realized her offbeat ways had rubbed off on the horse. He suspected she had that effect on everyone whose life she touched.

With a scowl, he turned and stepped off the brick divider. He walked away from the crowd, away from the feeling of impending doom that had settled around him.

Lanie had been so aware of Reece's eyes on her, of the hard scowl that had glazed over his face, and of the fact that he'd left so abruptly, that she almost failed to notice she was nearing the judges' stand. Jerking her attention back to the task at hand, she stopped and turned to face the woman and three men seated on the platform. Hoping Winnie would remember the trick she'd been taught, Lanie grasped the halter and gave the signal. Amazingly, on the second try, Winnie extended one tiny blue hoof and lowered her head in an exaggerated bow.

Lanie gave the little horse a hug and led her beside Etta's Eatery. Borrowing a bucket from Etta, she filled it from the outside tap. While Winnie quenched her thirst, Lanie removed the signs and unhooked the wagon. She left them on Etta's large back porch for safekeeping.

A crowd of children quickly gathered around Winnie. Lanie smiled at the kids as they argued over whether Winnie was actually a pony and whether she'd bite. Their interest in the horse quickly waned when their parents asked whether they wanted to buy hot dogs or Brunswick stew.

Lanie had no sooner led Winnie to the shade of the courthouse lawn when she was approached by a teenage girl who wanted to pet the horse. The girl's black hair sprouted wildly from a loose ponytail at the base of her neck. Her brown flowered-print dress flowed loosely over her doughy body. One of her sneakers was untied. Her smile, though friendly, was little more than a contorted grimace.

"I ride," she said. Her words were guttural, almost unintelligible. The black-haired girl lifted her knee as she turned toward Winnie. With horror, Lanie realized what she intended to do.

Reece stopped at the edge of the courthouse lawn and watched Lanie swiftly but gently catch the girl's arm in an effort to restrain her. He debated whether to intervene. Debbie Hicks was strong, and she could be a handful when frustrated.

While he hesitated, Lanie covered Debbie's hand with her own and patiently showed her how to rub behind the horse's ears. Reece marveled at Lanie's ability to make friends with everyone she encountered.

He tucked one of the two canned sodas that he'd bought in the crook of his arm and pocketed the change. Now Lanie was urging the girl to feed Winnie a handful of grass. When the horse's lips touched her fingers, the girl giggled and dropped her hand to her side.

Lanie laughed. It wasn't a malicious sound, but one of joy at shared fun.

Debbie's mother called out to her. Reece smiled when he noticed Lanie seemed as disappointed as Debbie to end their play.

Reece stepped forward and handed Lanie one of the drinks. While she popped the top, Winnie nuzzled his shorts pocket. He surrendered his butterscotch candy to the little urchin.

Lanie raised her soda can in mock salute. "Thanks. You're a mind reader."

"No," Reece admitted with a wry smile, "if I were a mind reader, I would've had you working overtime today to keep you from making a mockery of me."

Did he detect a flash of anger? If so, she quickly concealed it. Her lips were pressed into a thin line.

"Made a mockery of you?" she asked softly. "You mean, the way you made a mockery of me at the banquet last week?" She twisted Winnie's lead rope around her hand and made a fist.

Reece sighed. She was still out of torque over that. "Okay, so this—" he waved a hand to encompass her outfit and Winnie's streamers "—makes us even. Truce?"

He didn't know why he cared whether Lanie was still upset with him. Maybe they'd both be better off if they'd just agree to disagree. Yet, for some unfathomable reason, he had to know that she wasn't still angry with him.

Lanie unfisted her hand and ventured a smile. "Truce."

A feeling of relief washed over him. But his reaction unsettled him. Why should it matter to him whether he was in this wacky woman's good graces? How could he remain in control of his actions if he was seeking to please someone else? Especially if that someone was sure to wreck the orderly calm of his life.

The loudspeaker system squawked, and the parade spokesman began announcing honorable-mention awards. When he got to the second-place winner, he called Lanie's name. With a squeal of delight, she flashed a brilliant smile at Reece and trotted Winnie up to the platform to accept her trophy. Reece watched as she made Winnie bow for the crowd. When he realized he was smiling as broadly as Lanie, he knew he'd gone too far. Not only had he let himself care what she thought of him, but he'd committed the ultimate foolishness and let himself care for *her*.

She wound her way back through the throng, clutching the trophy to her star-studded chest. In a desperate act of self-preservation, Reece disappeared into the crowd.

He bought a hot dog at the concession stand in front of Tinsman's Auction Barn, then went behind the courthouse. The library bench was already occupied by an elderly couple, so Reece sat on the cement porch and let his legs dangle over the edge.

With fewer people on the back side of the square, it was quieter here. Reece relaxed as he ate his hot dog. His gaze wandered to the two women chatting by the water fountain. He immediately recognized Mrs. Parker, a friend of his mother's. The younger woman was about his age, with a luxurious mane of tousled blond hair and a petite body that wouldn't quit. Something about her nagged at his memory, and he tried to place the painstakingly made-up face.

The bite of hot dog formed a leaden lump in his mouth as high school memories swelled to the forefront. Jennifer Jordan. Reece swallowed hard, his appetite suddenly gone.

Jennifer had been his idea of the perfect girl. But she'd gone steady with Reece's best friend all through high school. Shortly after graduation they'd broken up, and she'd married someone else. A thousand times after that, Reece had called himself a chump for having been too "honorable" to make a play for his best friend's girl.

Something cold and wet touched his bare leg. Reece looked down to see a pregnant beagle begging for the rest of his hot dog. He tossed it to her and turned his attention back to Jennifer.

The years had been good to her, adding only enough pounds to flesh out the curves on her slim frame. She wore a crisp pink-and-white shorts jumpsuit that was clearly intended to emphasize her fantastic tan. When she laughed at something Mrs. Parker said, Reece noticed that her smile was as perfect as ever.

But more than her physical good looks, it was her quiet, demure ways that had held Reece transfixed.

Demure. Reece wondered if Lanie knew the meaning of the word. With that flag outfit she was wearing today, demure would be the last word he'd think of to describe her. No, he'd never seen Jennifer wear jungle prints or the bold, dynamic colors Lanie seemed to prefer.

Mrs. Parker caught him staring at Jennifer and said something to her. The next thing he knew, they were walking toward him. Reece hopped down from the porch ledge and greeted them both warmly.

"Reece Masardi, how *are* you?" Mrs. Parker asked as she slipped an arm affectionately around his waist. "How's your mama?"

Reece returned her hug with a one-armed squeeze. "I'm fine. And Mom's around here somewhere."

Jennifer waited quietly—demurely—until Mrs. Parker got around to reintroducing them.

"You remember my niece, don't you? Jennifer's moving back to Bliss now that she's...divorced." Mrs. Parker's voice dropped on the last word.

Jennifer didn't seem to mind her mentioning it. She held out her hand for him to shake, and he noticed how small and frail it felt in his. She had no grip. Reece let go and shoved his hands into his back pockets.

"I'm sorry to hear about your breakup," he consoled, "but Bliss is fortunate to have you back."

"Thank you." She cast her eyes becomingly downward. Reece thought her action a bit too calculated. "It wasn't much of a marriage, actually," she confessed. "We always did things his way, and when I told him I wanted children, he refused." She shrugged one shoulder. "So we parted ways."

"It's just as well," said Mrs. Parker, "the way that man walked all over you."

An image of Lanie flashed through Reece's brain, her chin thrust upward in defiance and her hazel eyes clearly issuing a warning not to push her too far. No, he couldn't imagine anyone walking over Lanie. He grudgingly acknowledged that he admired her spunk, but he still thought she could take a few lessons from Jennifer and tone it down somewhat.

Annoyed with himself, Reece shook the vision from his mind. Here he was with the girl of his dreams—who had just announced that she was available—and he was thinking of Lanie. He was getting to be as wacky as Lanie.

They made small talk, and Reece learned that Jennifer was an elementary schoolteacher. A nice, conservative job, he thought, unlike working in a psychiatric clinic. An involuntary smile sprang to his lips at the thought of Lanie impersonating the Good Witch of the North. That must've been a hoot.

". . . so anyway, she'll probably end up staying home tonight because she's too much of an old-fashioned girl to ask anyone herself," Mrs. Parker was saying.

Jennifer batted her lashes prettily. "Oh, Aunt Judith, don't embarrass Reece. Besides, he probably already has a date for the dance."

Dance. Reece remembered that the Bliss Festival Dance would be held at the Memorial Building tonight. He hadn't been to the dance in three years. He'd certainly make a whopper of a comeback with Jennifer to accompany him.

All he had to do was ask her—her eyes pleaded with him to do so—but something held him back.

"You know, Reece, I had the biggest crush on you all through high school." As if embarrassed by her disclosure, she dropped her gaze and smoothed a pleat on the front of her jumpsuit.

"You did? But you were going with Stevie." A warmth crept up Reece's collar. After all that soul-searching and agonizing over his decision to do the honorable thing and leave his best friend's girl alone, here she was—fifteen years later—telling him she'd had a crush on him. "Why didn't you say something then?"

"I . . ." She toed the dirt with her pink sandal. "I didn't want to hurt Stevie's feelings. He was such a nice guy."

Reece shook his head. None of what she was saying made sense. "But you two broke up after graduation."

"It wasn't my idea. Stevie wanted to date around before we made a commitment."

"Well, that was his loss," Mrs. Parker interjected. She turned to Reece. "Stevie took so long getting around to popping the question, Gordy Johnson jumped right in and beat him to it."

He'd thought Stevie foolish at the time to risk losing such a pleasant, attractive girl as Jennifer. But now it was beginning to make sense. On their double dates she'd always gone along meekly with whatever Stevie wanted to do. Reece had thought Jennifer conservative and easygoing. Now he saw her for what she really was—bland and opinionless.

If he wanted her, all he had to do was say so. It would be easy to mold her into the kind of mate he'd always wanted. If he wanted her to stay home and raise a houseful of kids, she would readily give up the teaching career she said gave her so much pleasure. And she'd probably be just as compliant in the bedroom.

Lanie would probably like Jennifer. Lanie seemed to like everybody, faults and all. She'd been so accepting of Debbie Hicks, even after the girl had almost unwittingly hurt Winnie. Why couldn't he accept Lanie as readily?

Jennifer was exactly the kind of girl he'd always pictured himself settling down with. But in the past month or so it seemed his plans had gone topsy-turvy.

Winnie squealed with indignation. Heads turned. Sheepishly Lanie relented and gave the horse the point of her ice-cream cone. Just that small bite wouldn't hurt her, she hoped. "Garbage gut," she muttered.

At the water fountain, she drank her fill, then cupped her hands and filled them for Winnie.

"Well, Reece, if you want to take her to the dance, you'd better ask her quicklike before somebody else snaps her up," a woman said.

Lanie looked up to find Reece with one of the prettiest women she'd ever seen. With that blond hair and deep tan, she looked like a California beach girl. Her hands clasped in front of her, she seemed hopeful as she waited for Reece's response. Judging by looks alone, she appeared to be a perfect match for him.

Lanie didn't know her, but she recognized the older woman who'd made the comment. Childishly she felt a twinge of jealousy. No, it was more than a twinge. The green poison flooded her veins.

She ought to just walk away and pretend she hadn't overheard a single word. Something compelled her to stay, sipping water to prolong her time at the fountain. She would probably regret her decision, but perhaps by knowing he was interested in other women and actively dating, she could more easily accept that they were not meant to be.

Reece hadn't seen Lanie. She was surprised to hear him stammer and clear his throat. Only a eunuch would turn down a date with someone who looked like that.

Reece was no eunuch. His kisses had left no doubt about that.

"What's the matter, you got somebody else?" the older woman asked.

He cleared his throat again and muttered something unintelligible. Then Lanie knew. In the short time she'd known him, she'd never seen him at a loss for words. He was trying to find a way *not* to ask the woman out.

Boldly Lanie walked up to Reece and slipped her arm familiarly through his. "Reece, honey, I've been looking all over for you," she gushed. She smiled at the two women. "Aren't you going to introduce me to your friends?"

After his initial shock, Reece's features registered relief. He smiled his thanks and began the introductions.

Lanie had already met Mrs. Parker at church, and they reacquainted themselves. Prepared for the jealousy that she expected to take root at meeting Reece's high school chum, Lanie was surprised when that emotion gave way to regret.

Regret that Jennifer claimed a part of Reece's life that she would never know. And regret that she couldn't summon up any animosity toward this gorgeous blonde with the genteel manner and genuine friendliness.

In a matter of minutes, Lanie was agreeing to take Winnie for show-and-tell day in Jennifer's first-grade classroom.

Lanie's knuckles were warmed where Reece absently rubbed the back of her hands with his thumb. The reactions the simple gesture aroused were too intimate to experience in public—in front of Reece's potential, or possibly ex, girlfriend. Licking her dry lips, Lanie tried to cover her discomfiture by reverting to babbling.

"I hope we'll see you at the dance tonight," she told the women. "You *are* coming, aren't you? Reece and I have been looking forward to it all week. Haven't we, dear?"

Reece just grinned down at her with glazed eyes. Lanie knew that, once again, she'd overstepped her bounds. Someday her impulsiveness would get her into a heap of trouble. When Reece unhooked her hand from his arm and clasped his fingers through hers, she was thankful today was not that fateful day.

Mrs. Parker and Jennifer murmured their goodbyes. But before they could beat a hasty retreat, a stray beagle jumped up against Jennifer, leaving dark smudges on her pastel jumpsuit.

Jennifer cried out and stepped back to avoid further damage. Waving away the dog with one hand, she brushed at the dirt with her free hand.

"Oh my," said Lanie as she picked up the friendly pooch. "I hope that mark will come out."

Mrs. Parker immediately took control of the situation. "Come along, Jennifer. Let's get some cold water on that before it becomes a permanent stain."

Holding the dog in her arms like an infant baby, Lanie watched them go. "Jennifer's very nice. You must be crazy not to want to date her." Reluctantly she added, "She seems to be just your type."

"Yeah," said Reece, and Lanie's heart dipped at the wistful tone in his voice. "I once thought she was my kind of girl. But not anymore. Besides," he said, slinging an arm around her shoulder, "I already have a date for tonight. And I've been looking forward to it all week."

Trying to ignore the comfort she found in the circle of his arms, Lanie rubbed the dog's exposed belly and smiled as its hind foot twitched in pleasure. "Reece, about that dance date thing—I was just trying to help you out. After all, isn't that what office managers are for?" She smiled up at him as they strolled toward the sheep-shearing pen. "I never planned to hold you to it."

"But I plan to hold *you* to it."

For all of about three seconds, Lanie let herself enjoy the sensation of victory over the impeccable blue-eyed blonde. But then she reminded herself that Reece was only offering to take her to the dance out of a sense of honor, and maybe a little bit of gratitude for taking him off the hook with Jennifer.

"Oh, sure, you just want me to be your bodyguard," she quipped.

"You wouldn't lead me on and then let me down, would you?"

Lead him on? Let him down? Did he really *want* to spend the evening with her? And what, she silently asked herself, about their pact to keep things platonic between them?

"Reece, as one *friend* to another, I think I should remind you about our agreement."

As enticing as his offer was, she knew that only harm could come from a romantic evening with this man. Reece needed a settled, dependable woman who could give him an uneventful family life. For the life of her, she didn't know why he had turned down the opportunity to renew his relationship with Jennifer. He could do much worse.

Like getting entangled with someone like herself. She certainly wasn't settled or dependable. And life with her would always be far from uneventful.

The dog in her arms made little grunting noises, and Lanie continued rubbing its belly to quiet it. Reece slid his hand to the back of Lanie's neck and steered them to an empty bench behind the library. Children and their parents passed by on their way to the carnival rides at the rescue squad grounds while Winnie cropped the grass that sprouted beside the metal bench's claw feet. Reece sat quietly for a moment before saying anything.

Finally he said, "Why don't we just forget about that agreement?"

Chapter Nine

Going to the dance with Reece went against Lanie's better judgment. But that was true of many of her actions, especially where Reece was concerned. The old pink truck was acting up again, so Lanie drove them to the Memorial Building in her compact foreign car whose name she couldn't pronounce.

When pressed for an explanation, Reece said little more than his initial suggestion to "forget about that agreement."

Stealing a glance at him in the darkened room, Lanie noticed that he seemed more at ease than he had been earlier in the day. In fact, he seemed more content than he had since she'd first met him. Reece called out greetings to friends at other tables and introduced Lanie to those who stopped to chat. She was surprised that he didn't mention she was his employee. Maybe he didn't want people to think he fraternized, she decided.

The band, a local group that played mostly rock-and-roll oldies and a little country and western, was still warming up.

"What's the harp for?" Lanie asked Reece.

His arm lay across the back of her chair. Lanie found herself acutely aware of his nearness. If she leaned back, she felt the caress of his touch against her shoulder, yet leaning forward would put her too intimately close to the man who turned her insides to mush.

Her dilemma worsened when he angled his chair toward hers and held her captive with his chocolate-brown gaze. A hint of amusement played around his mouth, and Lanie wished—not for the first time—that she didn't have to work so hard to keep from kissing him.

"You don't know?" he asked.

"If I knew, would I be asking you?" she responded sweetly.

His lips curled upward in a sly grin. Lanie almost wished she hadn't asked. Reece searched through the mingling crowd and leaned so close she could feel his breath on her cheeks.

"See that lady in the black dress?"

Lanie followed the line of his pointed finger to the middle-aged woman in a black, floor-length gown. She was easy to spot since everyone else in the room was casually dressed.

"Yes."

"That's Barbara Gardner. If you see her walking toward the harp, come find me and I'll show you what it's for."

"Can't you just tell me?"

Reece grinned again, broader this time. It was an expression that made Lanie feel like a canary being watched by a cat. "Not really," he said. "You need to see a demonstration to know what it's all about."

Lanie wondered if that were true, but she knew she wouldn't get any more out of him.

"Here they are, Dot. Come sit down before you have a conniption." Walter pulled out a chair for her, then took a seat beside her. "Well, come on. What are you waiting for?"

Dot blushed. "I don't know how to tell them."

"Then, *show* them."

Slowly, shyly, Dot lifted her left hand from her lap and spread her fingers on the table. A pear-shaped diamond winked from the simple gold ring on her finger.

Lanie gasped. The announcement was a surprise, but she instinctively knew Dot and Walter would live out their lives together, happy in each other's company. In the short time she'd known them, Lanie had grown very fond of the older couple. She considered Dot a special friend and could think of no better man for her to marry than Walter Pace.

Dot was strangely low-key about her announcement, and Lanie realized she was waiting for Reece's reaction. "Walter wants the Reverend Carlton to marry us next month," Dot said softly. "I hope you approve, Maurice."

Reece's playful mood vanished the moment he saw the engagement ring on Dot's finger. His face expressionless, almost serious, he sat across from his mother, taking in the news. Then he pushed his chair back, got up and walked to the other side of the table.

Please, Lanie thought, *please don't spoil Dot's happiness.* She remembered how Reece had spent hours working on the pickup truck, trying to get it running again. He clung to the memory of the man who'd given him the old relic. Someday, she knew, he would have to let go of the past. Just as his mother had done.

Reece knelt beside Dot. For a long moment, he said nothing as he searched her face. The moisture in his eyes glittered like Dot's diamond. And then he threw his arms around her neck and kissed her cheek. Lanie removed the cocktail napkin from under her drink and dabbed her eyes with it.

After a moment, he sat back on his heel. "Of course I approve. You're a terrific lady, and Walter's lucky to have you." Reece kissed her again and moved to stand beside Walter. Grabbing the older man's hand in both of his, he said, "Welcome to the family."

Lanie danced a few fast numbers with Reece, but she declined on the slow songs, offering excuses of thirst, hunger or tiredness. Reece looked disappointed, but he didn't persist.

The fast dances were fun, and Lanie could divert her attention from Reece by watching the other dancers around them. But she knew that the moment she stepped into his arms she'd be a lost woman. Lost to the warmth of his touch and the feel of his hard body against hers. No, she couldn't risk setting herself up for what was sure to be a devastating fall.

She wondered what made Reece change his mind about keeping their friendship simply that. Friendship. Had he forgotten what he'd said about it being ridiculous for them to consider any other kind of relationship? He seemed to be suffering a temporary lapse in judgment. Perhaps he was deluding himself that, despite their differences, they could make a go of it.

But it could never work. Lanie would have to be strong enough for both of them to resist the magnetic pull that seemed stronger tonight than it had ever been.

The band struck up another fast tune, and several people hollered out in chorus, "Paul Jones!"

Reece wrapped one arm around her waist and hauled her back to the dance floor. Keeping time to the upbeat tempo, he rocked her and spun her until she was almost dizzy.

"Who's Paul Jones?" She had to shout to be heard.

"Not who," he shouted back. "What. We're dancing the Paul Jones. When you hear the whistle, get in line with the women and you'll go in a clockwise circle. The men will circle around the women in the opposite direction."

"Then what?"

"Then when the whistle blows again, you dance with whoever's nearest you."

"Oh." It didn't make sense, but the frantic pace of it was giddying. Although breathless, Lanie was thoroughly enjoying herself. She was beginning to get the hang of it when a whistle shrilled. Reece released her and nudged her toward where the women formed a haphazard line. Lanie broke in and held the hands of the ladies in front of and behind her. Trying to imitate their quick, shuffling steps, she performed her own version of clogging. Her stockinged feet were not as quick or graceful as some of the others, but Lanie was glad to see that there were some who appeared even more fumble-footed than she.

The whistle blew again, and this time Lanie cavorted with a red-faced teenager who sported the beginnings of a scraggly beard. Scanning the room over her partner's shoulder, she saw Reece smoothly gliding Lou Wertzle across the dance floor.

The whistle sounded twice more, and her next partner was the farmer who had goaded Reece at the banquet. Ed Lowell was probably no more than five years older than Lanie, but his leathery skin looked like it belonged on a man of at least forty. He grinned and pressed Lanie to his hard, rounded stomach before whirling her so fast her feet barely touched the floor. Mercifully the song ended before she reached the point of hyperventilating.

Her heart beating against her ribs, Lanie thanked her partner for the dance and tried to disengage herself from his viselike hold. The band struck up another number, and the lead singer began a good imitation of Elvis singing "Love Me Tender." Lanie tried again to squirm free, but Ed held her tighter.

He grinned down at her, displaying nicotine-stained teeth. "You don't think I'm gonna let a good dancer like you get away, do you?" With that, he pulled her with him as he jogged too fast to the slow love song.

Lanie was about to murmur an excuse about her tired feet when Reece tapped on her partner's shoulder.

"Man, you must be crazy." Ed pressed Lanie tighter, flattening her breasts against him, and turned his back to the intruder. Lanie considered stomping on his instep or kneeing him. She discarded those ideas when she remembered he was wearing leather brogues and she was shoeless, and at this close proximity her knee would be ineffectual.

Fortunately Reece was not easily shrugged off. Mocking Ed's steps, he danced behind the farmer and winked at Lanie.

"I hear you need some help putting up that new barn of yours," Reece said.

Ed slowed as he appeared to consider Reece's statement. Then he stopped and handed Lanie off. "It was a pleasure." Turning to Reece, he said, "Monday afternoon at four o'clock."

Before Lanie could follow him off the dance floor, Reece stepped in front of her, his arms opened for her.

She hesitated only a moment before accepting his unspoken invitation. Telling herself she'd be the worst kind of heel if she refused after he'd so gallantly saved her from being asphyxiated in Ed's death-grip, she moved into Reece's arms. In his gentle hold she felt safe from everything but her own flaming emotions. Why did forbidden fruit have to be so tantalizing?

"Thanks for the rescue," she murmured against his chest.

His hand tightened on the small of her back, just above where her black dress flared out into a succession of hot pink and neon green ruffled bands.

"We're even now."

Lanie knew he was smiling by the way his cheek moved where it rested against her temple.

"Besides," he added, "there's no way I'd let you slow dance with Ed Lowell after you'd been turning me down all evening."

"Kind of flattens the old ego, huh?"

He didn't respond in words, but his breath puffed against her hair in a soft, feathery laugh.

Moving slowly to the popular melody, they circled the crowded floor. Lanie knew she shouldn't be enjoying this so much. In the morning, without romantic music and dimmed lights to cloud her thinking, she'd look back on this moment and regret letting her impulses rule again. But, for now, she would let her body flow with his, feeling the vibrations of his chest against her sensitized breasts.

He was humming. Lanie closed her eyes. Just a few more seconds until the song was over, and she'd go back to being just his neighbor and office manager. His humming changed, and Lanie realized that, though barely audible, he was now singing the words.

Something about loving her, and that he always would.

Lanie's breath caught in her throat as she wished in vain that the words were meant for her. So what if, at that moment, he molded his body to hers in an embrace so sensual that she almost forgot they were on a public dance floor? For a brief instant, she found herself wishing they were someplace private so she could explore these strange, new sensations.

Quit kidding yourself, Lanie mentally chided. *It's just a song. He didn't mean anything by it.*

People often mouth the lyrics to songs without giving a thought to the meaning, she reminded herself. And even if Reece had been singing the words for her benefit, Lanie knew he was grievously wrong in doing so.

She was about to step away from him and flee to the safe, neutral territory of their table when the lights flickered once, then twice. Just before they went out for the third and last time, Lanie saw Barbara Gardner take her place on the platform. A second later, the room was black, and wisps of harp music floated around her.

When Reece's lips touched hers, all rational thoughts of keeping a "platonic relationship" and being "strong for both of them" evaporated from her head. Like Scarlett O'Hara, she'd worry about that tomorrow.

But tonight she'd give in, just one last time, to his mind-drugging kiss. Her hands clutched his waist, then roamed over the hard planes of his back. Her fingers ached to pull his shirt loose and explore the lean flesh of his bare torso. Pressing closer, she knew that Reece's desire was as strong as her own. His maleness throbbed against her femininity, and Lanie couldn't get close enough to the warmth he exuded.

She shifted in his arms and returned his kiss with a fervor that left no doubt of her need.

A wave of euphoria washed over her, filling her with a sense of peace. Of rightness. It was as if she had found her niche, and that special place was in Reece's arms. It felt as though, after a lifetime of searching, she'd found a home.

Agonizingly Lanie found herself being released from Reece's kiss and from his arms as the last strains of harp music faded away.

The paddle fans on the ceiling swirled humid air over her as the lights blinked back on. Though the room was still shrouded in semidarkness, Lanie felt sure her cheeks must be glowing like stoplights.

Standing apart from her, Reece gripped her hands in his. A damp tendril curled over his forehead, likening him to the man whose song he'd hummed along with. There was a faraway look in his eyes as he smiled down at her.

"That was one of our county's oldest traditions—the Kiss of Bliss." He let go of her hand and wiped the dampness from his forehead. The little Elvis curl now stayed obediently in place with the rest. "How was it?"

The room no longer swam around her, but the pounding hadn't quite left Lanie's brain. "Blissful," she breathed.

Reece relaxed into Lanie's passenger seat as Lanie pulled out onto the Courthouse Road. After three years of not attending the Bliss Festival Dance, he had to admit this was a great way to end the streak.

Elbows jutting out like bat wings, he clasped his hands behind his head. He was feeling so good, in fact, that he didn't bother to comment when Lanie turned the wrong way onto Courthouse Road. No need to spoil the moment. She'd soon realize that she was going the wrong way and correct her mistake.

Only a month ago, he would have wasted no time pointing out Lanie's error. Hell, a month ago, he wouldn't have considered taking someone like Lanie to the dance.

He smiled to himself when he considered the new, relaxed attitude that had come over him lately. When he stopped to consider it, his "new" frame of mind wasn't so new after all. Just three short years ago, before his father had gotten sick, Reece had been a lot like Lanie. The only difference was that the mischief he'd created had been intentional, whereas Lanie's was usually accidental.

Aware of the personality change that had begun with his father's illness, Reece had claimed it as a conscious decision. After all, he had done the responsible thing, compensating for his father's lack of good judgment. But now, after three years of playing the responsible son, Reece was beginning to see his behavior for what it really was.

He'd been hiding. He'd felt a need to remain in complete control of his behavior and emotions, subconsciously afraid that failure to do so would result in complete *loss* of control.

A memory of his father, driving aimlessly because he'd forgotten where he'd been heading, invaded Reece's thoughts. Irrationally Reece had abandoned the carefree ways of his younger days, as if by sheer will alone he could protect himself from his father's fate. The decisions he'd made, both conscious and subconscious, to change himself were with the feeling of "better safe than sorry."

Only, now, he was sorry he'd almost let the "new Reece" deny himself the chance of getting to know Lanie for who she really was. Looking beneath the wacky exterior, he could see that she was a genuine and loving woman. And unlike Jennifer Jordan, Lanie definitely had a mind of her own.

Maybe he could take a few lessons from Lanie. There was no reason he had to give up being a solid, dependable businessman. Nor should he have to forgo the pleasure of spontaneous fun. Lanie managed to combine both in her life. Why couldn't he?

And one sure way to infuse spontaneous fun into his life was to make Lanie a part of it.

Turning to look at her, he drank in the sight of her. She was the most intense person he'd ever known. Hunched over

the steering wheel, she peered into the blackness as they circled the courthouse for the second time.

"Lost?"

"Not me. I'm looking for the little beagle that was here
this afternoon. Do you see her?"

"Why?" Reece was surprised—and somewhat pleased—
to find that he wasn't losing patience with her over the unexpected response. Instead, he found himself *wanting* to get
involved in her latest adventure. Or misadventure.

"She wasn't wearing a collar. What if she doesn't have
enough to eat? And when the puppies are born, they'll need
shelter."

Reece resisted the urge to lay a comforting hand on her
shoulder. If he touched her now, he wouldn't want to stop.
"Since Etta's been complaining about her garbage cans being knocked over every morning, my guess is we might have
some luck behind the restaurant."

Lanie pulled the car onto the grass beside Etta's Eatery
and angled the headlights toward the back porch. Sure
enough, a small animal skulked from behind the garbage
can and crawled under the porch.

Reece got out and followed her to the back stairs where
she hunkered down beside the broken latticework skirting
the porch.

"Here, girl. Come on." Lanie extended a hand and made
little kissing noises with her lips.

"Be careful. She might bite if she's afraid."

"She's not afraid of me," Lanie said confidently. Her
voice rose to that funny soprano she'd used on the tadpoles
that day at his mother's pond. "You wouldn't bite me,
would you, girl? Come here."

Reece could hear the animal moving around under the
porch. He squinted into the shadows cast by the misaimed

headlights but couldn't see anything except a glimpse of white.

"Do you have a flashlight in your car?" he asked.

She nodded. "In the glove compartment."

Reece jogged the short distance back to the car. Sitting half-in and half-out of the compact car, he rummaged past the papers and owner's manual until his fingers closed around a cylindrical object.

Something brushed against his pants. Reece aimed the light down at his leg. The little dog, still obviously very pregnant, tugged at the leather tassle on his shoe. He chuckled softly. "How did you get past Lanie?"

He picked up the beagle and walked back to where Lanie was still kneeling. "Come on, girl," she pleaded. "I know you're in there."

Sure enough, it sounded like something was moving under the porch. Reece frowned.

"Lanie," he said, "look what I've got." He directed the flashlight beam toward the brown-and-black bundle tucked under his arm.

Lanie turned on her heel and looked up at them. "If you have the dog—" she spun back and peered again through the broken boards "—what's under the porch?"

Reece shone the light into the hole, and two angry eyes gleamed back at them. With horror, he realized the blaze of white he'd seen earlier extended down the creature's back and along the length of its tail. He cautiously backed away. "Good Lord, it's a polecat!"

The dog whined, and Lanie rose slowly. "Is that anything like a skunk?"

"One and the same," Reece concurred.

She backed away in as much restrained hurry as she could muster.

* * *

Lanie unloaded the refrigerator of most of its contents. "She can have *must-gos* tonight. I'll buy her some dog food tomorrow."

Reece glanced over her arm at the assortment of food on the kitchen table. "I don't think it's a good idea to give a pregnant dog Mexican food," he said.

"Mexican food?" She stopped mixing bologna pieces with an unidentified dish, and then laughed. "Oh, that! *Must-gos* are leftovers that 'must go.'" Lanie set the pan of food and a bowl of fresh water at the back door. The little dog ate ravenously while Reece restrained Winnie from moving in on her late-night supper.

Reece seemed in no hurry to go home. Lanie found herself reluctant to say good-night.

"I'm sorry I almost got us skunked," she said at last.

"A miss is as good as a mile," he said jovially.

Lanie did a double-take at the man who, just last week, would have used the opportunity to lecture her on the importance of caution. In fact, he hadn't once tried to deter her from her mission by mentioning the possibility that the dog could be carrying rabies. She made a mental note to have the vet check the dog thoroughly, first thing on Monday.

"Are you all right?" she asked.

"Yeah," he said with a grin. "Fine as frog hair."

Lanie waved away an errant moth and stepped out of the porch lamp's circle of light. Crickets chirped, adding an eerie element to an already magical night.

"I had fun at the dance," she said, illogically trying to think of a way to delay his inevitable departure.

Reece moved to stand beside her, and Winnie managed to wedge her way between them. "Thanks for driving," he said.

"You really ought to buy a new truck."

His only reply was a noncommittal "Mmmph."

Lanie absently stroked Winnie's mane. "You're going to hate me Monday afternoon when you're helping Ed Lowell with his barn."

Reece turned to her. Even in the feeble shadows, she could see the intensity of his gaze. "A few hours' work for a dance with the prettiest girl in the county? A fair trade, I think."

Instinctively she knew he was sincere. But, factually, she knew that if he'd wanted to dance with the prettiest girl in Bliss, he could have asked Jennifer and spared himself some work. An awkward silence followed.

"Well—"

"Do you—"

"You go first," Lanie said after they shared a bit of embarrassed laughter.

"On nights like this, I used to sneak out the window after my parents sent me to bed. Wanna see where I went?"

"Can I get there in these?" Lanie pointed to her strappy sandals.

"No problem."

Reece reached for her hand and led her across the road to his mother's house. On the patio, he fumbled under a lawn chair cushion for the back door key. He let himself into the house and returned with a patchwork quilt and two cans of cola.

Lanie followed him around the pond, their only light a pale moon and thousands of glittering stars. When they came to a small clearing on a gentle slope overlooking the pond, Lanie helped him spread the blanket on the ground.

"When I was ten," Reece said as he settled himself down and popped the top on his soda, "it was too much trouble to sneak a blanket out the window. Every time Mom did the laundry, she fussed at me for getting grass stains on my skivvies.''

Lanie sat down beside him and studied the strong line of his throat as he tipped his head back and took a swig of his drink.

"And Dad always told her to 'quit harping on the kid.'" Reece grinned in remembrance. "I think he knew."

Lanie smiled, warming in the knowledge that he was again sharing a part of his past with her. It almost compensated for not having known him those many years ago. But then, out of the blue, that gut-gnawing feeling came back. A vision of Reece and Jennifer in this very spot—probably kissing, or whatever—pushed its way into her mind.

"Have you brought many girls here?" She regretted the question as soon as it came out of her mouth.

Reece appeared unbothered by her nosiness. "Lots," he said, leaning back on both elbows so he could study the night sky.

Lanie's soda turned to concrete in the pit of her stomach.

"Whenever my cousins visited, we had a picnic right here. And a couple of times, when I baby-sat the Vickery twins, I brought them here and taught them how to fish."

The concrete melted a little. But Lanie had to know for sure. "Did you ever bring any girlfriends to this spot?"

Reece rolled onto his side, one knee raised and his right hand bracing himself on the quilt. His posture reminded her of the time he had removed her splinters and then made himself comfortable on her bed. She tried to push the memory from her mind, because that was the night he'd kissed her for the first time. If she started dwelling on such thoughts now, she'd lose what remained of her rationality. No, there was no need in complicating matters by thinking with her glands. Unfortunately it was probably too late.

"No. During the day, this little clearing was a great spot to fish or build forts with my friends. It's kind of strange, but at night it seemed like a totally different place. This was where I came to do my thinking . . . and dreaming. I didn't want to share that with anyone."

"Not even Jennifer?" Lanie sat up a little straighter, aware of how ridiculously prim she must look but unable to relax.

"Not even Jennifer." Reece grew quiet.

Lanie shouldn't have asked him such a personal question. She was about to apologize when he spoke again. His voice was warm and husky.

"Given half a chance I would've married Jennifer."

Lanie didn't want to hear this. But she'd asked for it, so she would listen politely. And try not to cry. She twisted the metal tab on her drink can.

"My best friend was dating her at the time," he continued. "Looking back, I think it's probably the best thing Stevie ever did for me." Reece picked a blade of grass off the quilt and idly grazed it over Lanie's knee.

"Why do you say that?" she asked. Why must her voice suddenly come out so strained?

"He kept me from making the biggest mistake of my life."

"I liked her. And I was surprised you didn't want to go out with her. You seemed so right for each other." Why was she saying this stuff? Whose side was she on?

Her own, she reminded herself. For once, the rational portion of her brain was ruling. And, for once, she must encourage it.

"Fifteen years ago, I would've thought the same thing. Hell, ten *weeks* ago, I would've thought so." Reece sat up so his face was level with hers. "But today I realized I don't want her. Or anyone like her."

With the crook of his finger, he lifted her chin, forcing her to look at him. Forcing her to face a truth that she wasn't prepared to hear.

"I want someone who turns a boring day into an adventure, just by being there. I want someone who follows her heart instead of her head. I want *you*, Lanie." Reece moved closer, his knees touching the side of her thigh. "Deep down, I knew I wanted you the day you came busting into my house, demanding a gravy strainer."

"I still feel stupid about that," she apologized.

"You shouldn't," Reece insisted. "It's a perfect example of who you are. You're funny and caring, and you fly by the seat of your pants. But in spite of all that, you're also one of the most organized people I know. You're a complete contradiction, and that's what I love about you." Reece caught her hand in his. "That's why I love *you*."

Concrete butterflies clanked against the sides of Lanie's stomach. Reece was supposed to be the clearheaded one. Couldn't he see the mistake he was making?

"Reece, I—I don't know what to say."

"Just say you love me, too."

"Reece, you're so reliable, and I...well, as you said, I fly by the seat of my pants. You've got to admit, we don't exactly make a matched pair."

Reece laughed softly and made matters worse when he moved behind her to cradle her between his legs. His chin resting on her shoulder, he nuzzled her neck. Lanie was secretly grateful he couldn't see the tears forming in her eyes.

"You know," he said, his voice unusually tender, "in some ways we're complete opposites. But that's not so bad. We'll balance each other out. Who knows—if we get married someday, our kids will grow up to be normal and well adjusted." Reece squeezed her, and Lanie resisted the urge to relax back into his arms.

His declaration of love was a dream come true and a nightmare all rolled into one. She felt like the luckiest girl on earth to be wanted by this solid, rugged country boy. But she also felt like the lowest kind of life form for what she was about to do to him.

The tree toads chorused, their throaty croaks swelling in volume until they almost drowned out her words with their ruckus. Lanie wondered if any of the voices belonged to the pollywogs she and Reece had saved.

The can tab popped off beneath her agitated fingers. Lanie dropped it into her now empty container.

"Reece, you are the sweetest man I've ever met." *And I love you with all my heart,* her insides screamed, but she dared not utter the words. "I wish I could follow my heart, but I care for you too much to hurt you. That's why I must listen to my head this once." Reece had gone back to fidgeting with the blade of grass. "That's why we mustn't get involved."

Lanie followed his gaze to the pond. Moonlight rippled on the water, and fish surfaced to feed on night bugs. She looked back at the man who had brought her so much happiness in such a short time. Underneath his stoic expression, she could see the little boy aching inside.

"Damn," she whispered. "Pardon me."

If he was hurting now only half as much as she, then his heart must surely be breaking in two. She hated hurting him like this, but it was better to inflict a little pain now than a lot later.

Lanie rose to her knees and kissed his cheek. Her lips tingled from the touch of his sandpapery jaw.

"You deserve somebody better than me."

Reece didn't move as she got up and walked around the pond toward her house.

Chapter Ten

Reece left work early on Monday to fulfill his promise to Ed Lowell. Lanie spent the day avoiding Reece, holing up in her office and immersing herself in paperwork. At lunchtime she posted a lost-and-found flier at Etta's Eatery in an effort to find the beagle's owner, and then went home to check on the dog.

Guiltily, Lanie noticed that Reece got home from working on Ed's barn long after dark. Not that she was watching for him. It was the truck's backfiring that drew her attention to his arrival. He got it halfway up the driveway when the old clunker popped like gunfire, then shuddered and groaned to a standstill.

The next morning his truck remained where it had died. Lanie considered asking if he needed a ride to work, but drove away when she saw him walking across the road to Dot's house. He was probably going to borrow her fancy new car again.

Lanie cursed the circumstances that brought her into daily contact with Reece. They couldn't go on avoiding each other this way. Sooner or later they'd have to drop their defensiveness and get back to normal. Whatever normal happened to be.

Lanie sighed as she unbuckled Winnie from the seat belt and led her into the store. The horse nosed around as if searching for Barney, and Lanie tried to distract herself by compiling a list of sale items for the newspaper ad. It wasn't until Winnie shrilled a welcoming neigh and took off in hot pursuit of the gray cat that Lanie realized Reece had entered the room. Dot was right behind him.

"Elaine, dear, Maurice told me you'd been up to your elbows gathering last month's sales tax figures. Let me give you a hand."

Lanie glanced up at Reece's expressionless features and handed Dot the pile of untallied sales slips. "Thanks," she said. "It would be so much simpler if we had all this information on a computer."

"It's no bother at all." Dot took the papers to Reece's desk and separated them into neat stacks. "You can repay me by going with me to town tomorrow evening to shop for a wedding dress. You have such a lively taste in clothes, and I'd like you to help me pick out something young-looking." Dot pointed a pencil at Lanie and laughed. "I don't want Walter to think he's getting an old frump."

Lanie agreed to go with her elderly friend, taking the remark about her fashion style as a compliment. Even so, she felt conscious of Reece's eyes sweeping over her, taking in the bright Indian-print top that looked like overlapping triangles of cloth with openings for the neck and arms. Was it disapproval that registered on his face? If so, maybe he had come back to his senses since Saturday night and realized how incompatible they were. Somehow that knowledge did nothing to relieve the ache that throbbed from the depths of her soul.

Reece stood at the door, looking strangely uncomfortable. Lanie turned back to the sale ad, trying to ignore his presence, trying to ignore the odd undercurrent that flowed through the room.

"Mom," he said, "if you're in no hurry to leave today, I'd like to borrow your car to run some errands."

"Feel free," Dot answered. "Just make sure you're back in time to take me to the lawyer's office before it closes. If you don't have any objections, I'd like to trade deeds on our houses."

"Why on earth would you want to do that?"

"It was Walter's idea. We'll be travelling much of the time, and we can't use four bedrooms and all that land." Dot's voice had risen to an excited pitch as she discussed her plans. Now it took on a tone of coyness. "But if you would just settle down, you could fill up those bedrooms in no time."

Lanie stiffened in her chair. If the old matchmaker had started this discussion within her range of hearing to try to influence her, it wouldn't work. Dot's logic behind trading houses only served to remind Lanie why marriage to Reece couldn't work. Pretending not to have overheard, she rose from her chair and returned the price sheets to the filing cabinet.

"Thanks, Mom," said Reece. "Now all I have to do is find the right girl. Someone who'll say yes."

Lanie decided this would be a good time to help restock the shelves. She turned to leave the office, but Reece was lounging in the doorway, his arm stretched across the opening to block her exit.

"How about you, Lanie?" Reece said lightly. "Have you got any plans for the next, say, fifty or sixty years?" When she hesitated for an appropriate reply, he added, "I'll give you time off with pay to get the blood test." Even, white teeth gleamed from between his firm, sensual lips.

Why was he doing this? She'd already told him in very clear terms how wrong they were for each other.

"Oh, Maurice! Let's make it a double wedding ceremony," Dot exclaimed. "That is, if it's okay with you, Elaine."

Lanie made the mistake of turning to Reece for support. He reached into his wallet and pulled out a credit card. Handing it to Lanie, he said, "While you're out shopping with Mom tomorrow night, pick out a bride's dress for yourself." Ignoring her resistance, he grinned and pressed the plastic into her hand, closing her fingers around it. "I like virginal white."

The highway referendum vote turned out to be a disaster, with the public voting in favor of it.

"I just don't understand why they want it," Lanie complained to Dot as they browsed through a rack of dresses. "Bliss County is perfect the way it is now. Why ruin it by encouraging growth?"

"Because lots of folks want the best of both worlds," Dot explained. "The beauty and spaciousness of the country and the conveniences of the city. Can't blame 'em, myself. What do you think of this dress?"

Lanie nodded her approval of the pale blue lace-over-taffeta gown. "Well, maybe I'll have a few years before they change our zoning from agricultural to residential. Then I'll worry about moving again."

"The only place you'll be moving to, honey, is across the road with Maurice." Dot gave her an affectionate squeeze. "I always wanted a daughter."

"You know, Reece was just teasing."

Dot shook her head and led her to the junior-size dresses. "Maurice wouldn't tease about something as serious as marriage. If he wants something—or *someone,* in your case—he won't stop until he gets it. Now, here's a pretty white satin in your size. Do you think it'll clash with mine?"

It had been three weeks since Lanie managed to get out of the store without buying a bridal dress. But that didn't stop Dot from mentioning the upcoming wedding plans at every opportunity.

Reece, on the other hand, said nothing further about it. He was polite, but distant, as his attention seemed to be elsewhere. He ordered a large shipment of fencing materials and spent much of his spare time on the property behind his mother's house.

That was all right with Lanie since she was preoccupied with trying not to trample any of the six squirming puppies. Reece came over to see the newborns and asked if she planned to keep them. Lanie loved cuddling the babies, but she dared not keep even one since she feared it might find its way to the road and get hit by a passing car. No one had responded to her fliers, so Reece told her the beagle must have been a drop-off.

"People—usually from the city—bring their unwanted animals out to rural areas like Bliss," he said, "and drop them off on the side of the road, hoping someone like you will find them. More often than not, they're injured, get sick or starve to death."

Lanie understood how the little dog must feel. Lanie, too, had been pushed out of her home in the suburbs and had come here looking for a place to call home. Like the dog, she and Winnie wouldn't be able to stay here long before having to find another sanctuary.

Lanie had taken a snapshot of the puppies with their mother. She taped it and a small sign to the back of Violet's cash register.

"Free to good home, huh?" The deep voice rumbled close behind Lanie as she studied her handiwork. "Does the present owner come with them?"

She turned around and found herself face-to-face with Reece. It was almost October, yet his tan had faded little since the end of summer. His one concession to the cooler temperature was to wear jeans instead of shorts. His clean, outdoorsy smell reminded her of the intimate little clearing by the pond where they'd shared a blanket and Reece's childhood memories. Why did his mere presence send her mind on such tangents? As surely as he was standing in front of her, Lanie knew that time wouldn't diminish his effect on her.

Lanie pictured herself still working here five or ten years from now. He'd be married to a Bonnie or a Melissa, and pictures of her and their children would grace his desk and the wall on his half of the office. And, still, Lanie's heart would leap every time Reece entered the room, every time he looked at her as he did now with that one eyebrow cocked in question.

It was then that Lanie realized she'd have to find another job. Another boss.

"I—uh . . ." Here she was, stammering again like a bashful adolescent.

Mercifully he let her off the hook. "Have you seen our newest item in stock?" Leading her to a newly set-up display, Reece waved a theatrical hand over an assortment of grain and seed bags. Smaller than the fifty-pound bags that the farmers preferred, these came packaged in nostalgic floral patterns and old-fashioned brown burlap. The window behind the display sported a new pair of charming, country-style curtains made from the same type of fabric as the bags.

"I didn't order these. Where did they come from?"

Reece beamed at her, apparently delighted at her astonishment. "The dealer said we could sell these on a trial basis. If they do well, we'll keep stocking them in the smaller sizes for our home-owner customers."

"But—"

"Don't worry, you'll get full credit for the idea. And next week you'll be getting your new computer. I also took your suggestion about something else. Come on, I'll show it to you." He took her hand and led her to the back door, calling to Violet as he passed. "Would you and Howard hold down the fort? Lanie and I are going to take a long lunch."

"Reece," said Lanie, "I don't think they've had lunch yet."

Violet stepped ahead and held the door for them. "You two go right ahead." Her broad smile hinted that she knew something Lanie did not. "We'll be just fine," she assured them.

Outside, Reece opened the passenger door of a shiny red pickup truck with a camper shell on the back. He made an elaborate bow. "Please allow me to take you for a ride in the new, improved Masardi-mobile."

Lanie inhaled the new-car scent as he got in the other side. She ran a hand over the red vinyl seat.

"It's not as fancy as Mom's Jaguar, but it'll make a great shop truck. Oops, I almost forgot..." Reece appeared to be bubbling over in his excitement as he went back to the store and gave a piercing whistle. Winnie and Barney streaked toward him, and he let them into the back of the truck. "They wanted to go for a ride, too," he explained as he got back in and started the engine. He slanted a grin at her. "It even has a *'perndle'* indicator."

"It's automatic?"

"That was the least I could do for the mailboxes of our neighborhood."

Lanie stared at him in wonder. She'd been attracted to him from the first moment she'd met him. He'd seemed so befuddled the day she pounded on his front door. But she'd fallen like lead when she'd first seen the playful little boy under that gruff businessman exterior. And now that little boy was out in full force.

"This is a nice truck," she said. "But I'm still going to miss the old pink one." Oddly enough, she did miss it. She'd come to consider the dents and rust spots as character marks chronicling the events in Reece's life.

"Yeah, I'm going to miss her, too. But I planned for that. Take a look in the glove compartment."

Lanie opened the small door and pulled out an envelope full of pictures. Each photo showed a different angle of the old vehicle, inside and out.

"No truck will ever be like the old gal," he said, patting the red dashboard, "but at least this one's safer. You don't have to worry about Winnie falling out. And if you slide this glass over—" he reached back and pushed open the glass separating them from the animals "—it's almost like she's riding up front with you."

Lanie felt a hot prickling at the corners of her eyes as she considered his thoughtfulness. First the flowered feed sacks, and now this. She stared blankly at the photos. *Don't let him get too close*, she reminded herself. But even as she thought it, she knew the warning was too late.

Lanie watched the landscape go by, unaware of their surroundings until Reece turned onto Judestown Road. He pulled the truck into his mother's driveway—*his* driveway now—and came to a stop.

The outer corners of Reece's eyes crinkled like little star-bursts. "Well, don't just sit there," he said, hopping out of the truck. "come give me a hand."

He let the animals out and handed Lanie the patchwork quilt from the back of the truck. Then he extracted an oversized wicker picnic basket.

"Reece, what's going on?"

"Lunch. Can't you tell?"

His step was lively as he walked to the back of the house, and Lanie had to hurry to keep up. Then, as she passed the patio, she saw it. Framing the setting like a picture post-card, the new fence circled the pond, as well as the clearing and a small lean-to shed at the corner of a large portion of land behind the pond.

But unlike many of their neighbors' rustic fences, this one's broad, flat boards skimmed close to the ground and left little space between the horizontal slats. If it was in-tended to keep neighborhood children away from the wa-ter, Lanie decided it was a failure. The openings between the boards were too small for a child to scramble through, but a determined kid could easily climb over it.

"Reece, this looks so . . . picturesque."

"Come on. You've got to see it from the clearing."

Once there, he pulled a can opener out of the picnic bas-ket, followed by a can of cat food and a bowl full of horse feed.

"I'll be right back," he said and led the menagerie a short distance away. Lanie watched, amused, as he set the bowl down for Winnie, opened the can, and dumped the con-tents onto a paper plate for Barney.

When he came back, he set out a feast of sandwiches, chips, fruit and a bottle of wine. Lanie accepted her plate and took a bite of her sandwich. Peanut butter and jelly.

"Why are you doing this?" she asked.

Reece wiped a bread crumb from his mouth with the back of his hand. "They say the way to a woman's heart is through her stomach."

"That's 'a *man's*' heart," she corrected.

"I believe in equality of the sexes."

The dimple in his left cheek deepened. With a sinking feeling in her gut, Lanie knew that although Reece hadn't talked about marriage since he'd jokingly offered her his credit card three weeks ago, he didn't consider the matter settled. She remembered what Dot had said about him. *He won't stop until he gets what he wants.* And from the hungry look in his eyes, it was clear he wanted her.

Reece poured the wine into a paper cup and handed it to her. When she finished, he refilled it for her.

"Are you trying to get me drunk?"

"Whatever it takes."

Lanie set the cup down. She needed to be clearheaded when dealing with him—a near impossibility when he was close enough to touch.

Reece moved to her side, taking her left hand in his. He didn't meet her eyes, but stared down as he rubbed a thumb over her bare fingers.

"I don't know if I made this clear the last time we were here," he began, "but I want you to know how much I love you."

"Reece, don't—"

"Let me finish. In the short time we've known each other, I've learned a few things about you. That you're fun to be with. That you're a hard worker." He ran a hand over his brow, smoothing out the worry lines between his eyes. "I've also come to realize that your reason for refusing to be with me is the lamest excuse you could have come up with."

"We've been through all this before. I told you we're too different. And you mentioned wanting children—I'm not mother material."

"What you tell me and what you show me are two different things."

Lanie felt the heat of his gaze as he turned to her, studying her face with an intensity that made her want to turn away. But she was helpless in his brown-eyes trap.

"What I *see*," he said, "is the most nurturing woman I've ever met. I don't know many people who would have gone to the trouble you did to save those tadpoles."

Lanie gave a snort of derision. "So, I've got a soft spot for slimy amphibians. That doesn't mean anything."

"Do you want me to make a list?" Reece ticked them off on his fingers. "You tried to keep Weasel from seeing a fact of life you thought he wasn't ready for. You even risked getting kicked to keep him from being trampled by the cow." His voice softened as he added, "And who was it that washed my wounds and put medicine on my chest?"

"Anybody would've done the same," she insisted.

"Would *anybody* have sung a lullaby to a cow in labor?"

Lanie felt her cheeks grow warm. She hadn't realized he'd heard. He must surely think she was ridiculous. She met his gaze, but the only emotion she saw there was love. And maybe a little bit of frustration.

"Would *anybody* have made the sacrifices you've made just to keep your horse, or been as patient as you were with Debbie Hicks when she tried to ride Winnie? And I don't know too many people who search under porches at night because they're worried about a stray dog."

Lanie sighed. He presented a strong argument. But he was talking about now. What about the future?

Reece slipped an arm around her waist, bringing her close enough to kiss him if she wanted to. She wanted to, but she couldn't think about that now. She *mustn't* think about that.

"Tell me," Reece whispered. "Don't you think that sounds like 'mother material'?" He stroked her arm, sending warm sensations right to her heart. "Enough of your silly excuses. Now tell me you're madly in love with me and that you'll be my wife."

Lanie smiled back at him, but she still had reservations. "We're as different as two people can be."

Reece pointed to where Winnie and Barney lay sunning together. "So are they, but that doesn't stop them from being friends."

Lanie considered his words and her heart thumped wildly. In spite of her doubts and insecurities, she began to hope. Could it possibly work? Reece not only wanted her, he believed in her. With a love like that, how could they fail?

"I don't know how to cook very well," she warned, offering him one final opportunity to back out.

"I bet Mom could teach you if you offered to share your secret family recipe for spaghetti sauce." He brushed her hair back away from her face and let his hand linger at the sensitive spot under her ear. "I'm waiting for those three magic words."

"I'm still hungry?"

At that, Reece jumped up and lifted Lanie as easily as he hefted hay bales and sacks of grain. He carried her to the water's edge. "Tell me now, woman, or I'll throw you into the pond," he threatened. Despite the fierceness of his tone, his smile told her he knew the answer.

"Are you always this demanding?" she asked impishly.

"My horoscope said I should use my wits and force to get what I want today. I figured the peanut butter sandwiches wouldn't hurt, either."

By now he was standing knee-deep in water. He held her away from his chest as if preparing to drop her.

"I haven't got all day," he said. "Tell me now, or in you go!"

"I love you, I love you!" she said, flinging her arms around his neck. Lanie clung to him with a long-suppressed urgency and felt him tighten his hold on her.

"You'll marry me?"

He asked it tentatively as if he feared she might reject him again. He was so vulnerable, like a little boy, and it made her want to protect him. She wanted to shelter him from whatever harm or heartache might come along in his life. Or at least be there to share the burden. Even more, she wanted to share his joy—to be the cause of it.

"I'd be a fool not to marry you." Lanie kissed him and felt his heartbeat quicken against her ribs. He tasted like strawberry jelly and peanut butter and wine, and Lanie couldn't get enough of him. Reece returned her kiss with equal ardor.

He was trembling when he finally pulled away.

"I haven't shown you your wedding present," he said, his voice husky with passion. "Unless you'd rather forget about that and make love in the pond like a couple of alligators."

Breathless, Lanie surprised herself by saying she wanted to see the present when she really rather liked his second suggestion.

He set her down on the grass and led her up the hill toward the shed. They stepped inside and were greeted by a yearling horse whose head came no higher than Lanie's thigh.

Deep gold, with a thick blond mane and tail, the little animal was quick to make friends, nuzzling Lanie's pockets and then thrusting its nose into her hand.

"He's beautiful." Lanie stroked the horse's sleek sides. "But you shouldn't have. He must've cost you a fortune."

"If he makes you happy, he's worth every penny." Reece captured her waist and pulled her to him. "You know, beat-up old trucks don't last forever . . . and, unfortunately, neither do little black horses. With Tom Thumb's help there, you'll soon have a whole herd of mini Winnies. This way, your father's gift to you will never die."

"Oh, Reece." Unable to say more, Lanie hugged him, pressing her face against his soft, knit sweater. Even in his sadness over losing the truck his father had given him, his concern had been for her. And due to his thoughtfulness, she would be assured of always having a reminder of her father through Winnie's bloodline. Reece had turned her father's gift into a legacy.

Lanie squeezed him tighter, grateful not to have lost this wonderful man due to her own insecurities. Grateful that he loved her despite her Calamity Jane ways.

"Elgin Thurloe says little Tom here is good breeding stock and that you should call him anytime you have any questions." Reece played with a strand of Lanie's hair, wrapping it around his finger. "He also said he'd take those beagles off your hands. He needs some hunting dogs."

Lanie smiled as she remembered being so frightened by the wild, gun-toting man who'd thought they were with the highway department.

"Reece?"

"Mmm."

"What if the new highway brings so many subdivisions and new residents that we're forced to move away? Dot told me about a large subdivision that was built next to a pig farm. And then the new homeowners tried to change the zoning to force the farmer out. What if that happens to us?''

Reece laughed softly. The sound was deep and reassuring. ''Don't worry, nobody's going to force us out of our home. When we go to the administration office to apply for our marriage license, we'll ask the Board of Supervisors for an ordinance requiring larger lot sizes for new construction. I don't want our county to grow too fast, either, and this would help us stay rural.''

Reece lowered her head as if to kiss her, then stopped.

''Did you hear that?'' he whispered.

Lanie listened and heard nothing but the cool autumn breeze rustling the leaves above them. ''Hear what?''

''Harp music. I think it's time for the Kiss of Bliss.''

His lips were warm and tender, and Lanie felt her body melt against him. She welcomed the feel of his strong, capable arms around her.

Strong and capable. That described the man inside the body, as well. Lanie felt safe and protected. She'd found a wonderful, new home in his arms and never wanted to leave it.

''You know,'' she said, ''I never thought I'd say this, but I think it'll be fun traveling the highway to Bliss with you.''

Epilogue

"No, no, Maureen, you mustn't color on the baby's head with marking pens." It was all Lanie could do to hold back a laugh at her four-year-old's latest exploit.

"But, Mommy, he doesn't have any hair. I don't want people laughing at my brother."

Reece made no effort to suppress a smile as he lifted the infant out of the bassinet. "You sit there and rest," he told Lanie. "I'll see if I can wash this stuff off."

Lanie capped the brown watercolor pen and handed it to Dot to put away. Then she pulled Maureen onto her lap and hugged her tightly. "Otis will grow hair soon," she assured her.

Lanie extracted a promise that Maureen wouldn't color on her brother again. Lanie felt certain her daughter would live up to her promise, but wondered what other brainstorms she would act out in the future. Only now did Lanie realize what her father and grandmother must have gone through when she was growing up.

Reece walked back into the room, patting Otis's freshly scrubbed head with a plush towel. He sat down in a side chair, cuddling the boy to his broad shoulder.

Seeing her big, strong husband being so gentle with his tiny son made Lanie go all soft inside. Even after six years of marriage, she was still finding new facets to the man she loved.

"Why did you give the baby such an awful name?" Dot complained as she sat between Lanie and Walter on the sofa. She dropped a kiss on her granddaughter's blond curls.

"It's no worse than Maurice," Reece piped in.

"Besides," Lanie added, "what else would you name a boy born in an elevator?"

*   *   *   *   *

NORA ROBERTS

Love has a language all its own, and for centuries, flowers have symbolized love's finest expression. Discover the language of flowers—and love—in this romantic collection of 48 favorite books by bestselling author Nora Roberts.

Starting in February, two titles will be available each month at your favorite retail outlet.

In February, look for:

Irish Thoroughbred, Volume #1
The Law Is A Lady, Volume #2

In March, look for:

Irish Rose, Volume #3
Storm Warning, Volume #4

Collect all 48 titles and become fluent in

THE LANGUAGE of LOVE

From the popular author of the bestselling title
DUNCAN'S BRIDE (Intimate Moments #349)
comes the

LINDA HOWARD

COLLECTION

Two exquisite collector's editions that contain four of
Linda Howard's early passionate love stories. To add
these special volumes to your own library, be sure
to look for:

VOLUME ONE: *Midnight Rainbow*
Diamond Bay
(Available in March)

VOLUME TWO: *Heartbreaker*
White Lies
(Available in April)

Silhouette Books®

SLH92

Coming in February from

SILHOUETTE® Desire™

MAN OF THE MONTH

THE BLACK SHEEP
by Laura Leone

Man of the Month Roe Hunter
wanted nothing to do with
free-spirited Gingie Potter.

Yet beneath her funky fashions
was a woman's heart—and body—
he couldn't ignore.

You met Gingie in
Silhouette Desire #507
A WILDER NAME
also by Laura Leone
Now she's back.

SDBL

Take 4 bestselling love stories FREE
Plus get a FREE surprise gift!

WRITTEN IN THE STARS

WHEN A PISCES MAN MEETS A PISCES WOMAN...

Normally cool, calm and collected Pisces man David Waterman had never felt quite so hot-blooded! David didn't know why fellow Piscean Eugenia "Storky" Jones had "bought" him at a charity auction, but he planned on finding out—fast. Discover the delightful truth in March's STORKY JONES IS BACK IN TOWN by Anne Peters—only from Silhouette Romance. It's WRITTEN IN THE STARS!